The Most Terrible Murderer
and Other New
Sherlock Holmes Stories

By

Alan Dimes

Edited by David Marcum

Paperback ISBN 978-1-80424-719-8
ePub ISBN 978-1-80424-720-4
PDF ISBN 978-1-80424-721-1

Published by MX Publishing
335 Princess Park Manor, Royal Drive,
London, N11 3GX
www.mxpublishing.com

Cover design by Awan

For Les and Chris

Contents

The Adventure of the
Remarkable Worm

It was a beautiful, balmy evening, and I had thrown wide the windows of our sitting room at No. 221b Baker Street to let in the cooling breeze. I was content to do nothing more than sit back quietly and relax, but my fellow lodger was of a rather different humour. He'd had no cases for a full five days, and this idleness rendered him a difficult companion. The previous fortnight had been filled – indeed, crammed – with activity, which made his present lack of work the more frustrating. There had been the singular experience of M. Aristide Dubois, a merchant banker who had gone to bed in Paris and woken up two days later on the floor of the British Museum, and the case of the Thornton Heath Horror – to say nothing of the affair of Carew, the blind cracksman, which had so nearly cost us both our lives.

To do him justice, my friend had tried to fill the time constructively. He had spent a day on some malodorous chemical experiments, and then, perhaps sensing that the noxious fumes were making me uncomfortable, put his test tubes and Bunsen burner to one side and turned to the production of a first draft of a monograph he had long intended to write upon the specialised argots of various professions. For a few hours he made preliminary notes and consulted his scrapbooks, but then he stood up with a gesture of frustration and paced back and forth across the room, threw himself into his armchair, sat there for a short while, stood up again, and went over to the window.

He gazed down upon the street below for a minute or so, then turned and gave me a searching look, as if hoping to deduce something from my appearance and facial expression. As I hadn't left our rooms for some time, and felt relaxed and contented, I fear there was little for his genius to work upon.

He then went to the corner where he kept his violin, pulled the instrument from its case, and ran his bow across it, producing a gentle melody which I didn't recognise and presumed to be one of his own compositions. He continued in this vein for one or two minutes, and then concluded with a discordant cadenza. He threw the violin and bow down on a chair with an exclamation of disgust.

"A whisky?" I said, reaching across to the tantalus.

"No, thank you."

"A case will come, my friend. Depend upon it."

"I wish I shared your optimism, Watson. If I don't have work soon, then I shall be forced to seek stimulation elsewhere."

I confess I went a little cold at these words, for I had been struggling to help him rid himself of his addiction to cocaine, and knew that the little morocco case containing his hypodermic needle lay within easy reach in the drawer of his desk. My relief, then, when I heard the ringing of our doorbell may be readily imagined. Mrs. Hudson opened the door to our rooms to admit a little ferret-faced fellow in a grey lightweight cotton suit.

"Good evening, Mr. Holmes. Doctor."

It was Inspector Lestrade, the tenacious Scotland Yarder whom the consulting detective had assisted on many occasions.

Holmes smiled broadly.

"Lestrade, my dear fellow! Please, take a seat. Watson, perhaps the inspector would like a glass of whisky."

"Thank you very much," said the wiry little professional. "Don't mind if I do."

"And one for me, if you'd be so good. Now then, my friend," said Holmes when we were all seated with a drink in hand, "what brings you to our humble abode on this fine evening?"

"Well, Mr. Holmes, it's like this: Have you heard of Isidore Persano?"

"The journalist? I've read one or two of his articles. I can't say they were especially to my taste. What has he done?"

"Well, we've had our eye on him for some time at Scotland Yard. He lived in Paris for a while, and got himself quite a reputation there as a duelist."

"Ah, yes," said Holmes. "There was some contretemps in Pere Lachaise, I seem to recall."

"Yes. I don't know if that's why he left Paris, but since he's been in London, he's had a couple of very public altercations with men who later appeared to have sustained bullet wounds: Thomas Marlowe, another journalist, and Arnold Campbell, a hotelier. We couldn't pin anything on him on either occasion, but it seems highly probable that he had shot them in duels. Since dueling is illegal, neither man could press charges without incriminating himself."

"But what was the nature of these disagreements? They must have been serious to provoke such a reaction."

"Well, by all accounts, he's a bit of a strange chap. Spanish, I take it, by his name, with a proud and passionate nature. Claims to be thirty, but looks a good deal younger. Short, slim, a bit swarthy."

"Essential as these details are, you haven't answered my question: Why should he challenge these men to duels?"

Lestrade cleared his throat and looked somewhat uncomfortable.

"Persano has a very close relationship with the noted chemist, Dr. Thomas Poulteney, of 17 Margrave Villas, Stoke Newington. Dr. Poulteney is a bachelor of forty-five, and . . . well . . . ."

"And these two men suggested that the relationship between them is . . . *unnatural*?"

"You've hit on it, Mr. Holmes. Persano is also unmarried and lives by himself."

"Was there any indication of blackmail? You are aware, I'm sure, that homosexuality is at the root of the majority of such cases?" The whole subject was clearly a source of embarrassment to the Scotland Yarder.

"Thankfully I've had little to do with that sort of thing. There was no evidence of blackmail."

"So, Lestrade, what is there for me to do? Have there been fresh clues to these mysteries? Perplexing threads that you would wish me to untangle?"

"No, sir. It is the strange disappearance of Mr. Isidore Persano that we need your help to solve."

"Disappearance? Pray continue."

I offered Lestrade another whisky, and he accepted it gladly, taking a short sip of it before resuming his account.

"Persano was residing at 24 Monckton Street, just off the Strand. He came home two evenings ago at about six and asked the maid to bring him a cup of coffee before dinner. When she came into his study a few minutes later, she found him in a state of raving madness, hysterical and incoherent, and pointing at a matchbox that lay in front of him."

"A matchbox? Was there anything in it?

"I have it here, Mr. Holmes. See for yourself."

Holmes took the proffered Vestas box and pulled out the little cardboard drawer. I leaned over eagerly to see what it might contain. Inside lay a dead worm, but such a worm as I had never before seen in my life. It had a distinct head of a slate-blue colour, while its fat body was a darker blue mottled with red-and-yellow dots. "No one at the Yard had ever seen anything like it. I sent a man to Westminster Library and he looked it up, but it wasn't there. The Chief Inspector brought in the curator of the Kensington Museum, and he didn't recognise it either. It seems to be completely unknown to science."

"Fascinating. But the disappearance?"

"The girl went to the door and called a boy to fetch the nearest doctor. The man was just a general practitioner and didn't feel confident diagnosing a mental illness, so he just gave Persano a sedative and despatched a message to Colney Hatch to come and get him. They sent a carriage with an attendant. When they arrived at the asylum he was still asleep, so they locked him in a room and waited till he woke up so they could make a proper diagnosis. When they opened the door some time later, there was no one there. The room was completely empty. They contacted the Yard, so I took a couple of constables with me to search the building and grounds while I questioned the staff. My men did a very thorough job and found nothing."

"How often did the nurses check on him?"

"Once every quarter-of-an-hour."

"Any signs that the lock or hinges had been tampered with?"

"None at all. The windows were barred and the room was on the fourth floor."

Holmes pressed the tips of his long bony fingers together. "Did Persano's maid accompany him to the asylum?"

"No, Mr. Holmes. It was all she could do to get a lad to the nearest doctor. I spoke to her the next day and she was still shaken up, poor girl. She was relieved when I took that thing out of the house."

"How long has she been in Persano's employ?"

"Ever since he's been in London, apparently."

"Has he any other servants?"

"Not that I saw. She appears to be the only one that lives in, at any rate."

"What measures have you taken?"

"Well, the whole area's being combed for him, naturally, but I thought – "

"I am much obliged to you, Lestrade," said Holmes, standing up. "If you care to leave this with me, I will give it my fullest attention. Oh, by the way," he added as the inspector turned to the door, "would you mind if I take possession of that singular worm?"

"Certainly not," said Lestrade, handing over the matchbox. "As I said, we can make nothing of it down at the Yard. Well, good night, Mr. Holmes. Dr. Watson." When the street door had closed behind Lestrade, Holmes reached for his clay pipe and filled it with tobacco from the toe of his Persian slipper. "Well, Doctor, what do you make of it?" he asked through preliminary puffs of smoke.

I took a moment to think. "It seems to me that what we have here are two mysteries, and both are equally perplexing. What can be the connection between the two, other than that the same person is involved in both instances?"

"That is for us to discover. We must make a thorough investigation of both ends of the case, and as we progress they will doubtless throw light on each other. But give me your first impressions."

"The worm certainly seems to be of an exceptional character, but that is surely not enough to drive one insane at the mere sight of it. Fear of snakes is common enough. It even has a scientific name, *ophidiophobia*. But fear of worms – "

"*Vermiphobia*?" asked Holmes with a smile.

"Perhaps. It may exist, but it would be the first I have ever heard of it. That particular species of worm must have some special significance for Persano. But if it is unknown to science, how could he have seen one before?"

"How indeed? And what of his disappearance?"

"Supposing Lestrade's men didn't search as fully as they thought? From what I recall of Colney Hatch, it has a high wall and very secure gates. What if Persano is hiding somewhere in the building. Or the grounds?"

"If that's the case, then he'll be discovered very soon. I think, however, that you are being a little unfair to Lestrade and his men. They may be lacking in imagination, but we shouldn't cast aspersions on their diligence."

"Perhaps not. But then we have another mystery: The gates aren't only locked – they are guarded. How could he get through them? As for the locked door, I believe I have a solution to that." Holmes smiled again and sent a plume of smoke upwards.

"Pray tell."

"The windows were barred. Lestrade described Persano as small and slim, but even if he had been slender enough to get through the bars, the room was on the fourth floor. The walls are sheer."

"Ergo?"

"The door must have been unlocked, Persano freed, and the door locked again."

"Bravo, my dear Doctor! In this instance, the simplest and most obvious solution is the only one that will serve. But by whom was the door unlocked? Persano was asleep, so there was no opportunity for him to get a key. You will recall that I asked Lestrade if the maid had accompanied him. She hadn't, so who was there at the mental hospital who had any motive for being his rescuer? I shall think a little more on this matter and then have an early night – as should you, for I expect we shall have a busy day tomorrow."

The sun rose early the following morning, and after a light breakfast we set out by cab for Monckton Street. The traffic was fairly heavy, but our destination was no great distance from our lodgings, and we were there within twenty minutes. 24 Monckton Street was a narrow, elegant, terraced house with three floors. Holmes rang the bell, and a few moments later, it was answered by a pale-faced, petite young woman in a neatly pressed maid's uniform.

"Good morning. I am Sherlock Holmes, and this is my friend and colleague, Dr. John Watson. We have been engaged by the police to aid them in their investigation into the disappearance of your employer. I should like to come in and ask you some questions."

"Please do, sir," the maid said eagerly. "I shall do anything if it helps Mr. Persano." She showed us into a spacious drawing room. We seated ourselves in two of the four chairs.

"Please sit down, Miss – ?"

"Maisie Tiverton, sir."

"You are from Devon, I think, Maisie."

"Yes, sir, but how on earth did you know that?"

"Despite your years in London, you still retain slight traces of your original accent, and Tiverton is a very common name in the west of England."

I have mentioned before in these memoirs that while my friend had no great respect for the female sex in general, he was capable, when the occasion demanded, of treating individual women with care and consideration. I sat silently listening while he gently coaxed information from this girl, who was clearly still upset by the event which had overtaken her employer.

"Is Mr. Persano a kind master?"

"Oh yes, sir, one couldn't hope for a kinder. Very considerate, he is, sir. Very understanding and very generous."

"On the day of Mr. Persano's . . . *illness*, did anything come through the post for him? A package, perhaps, or a letter?"

"Oh no, sir. I was in all day and there was nothing."

"Were there any callers?"

"No, sir, not one."

"Thank you, Maisie. And now, could you show us to Mr. Persano's study?"

The maid's already pale face blanched still further. "Oh, please don't make me go in there again, sir!"

Holmes reached out and patted her little hand.

"You needn't come in with us. Just show us where it is."

She took us up two flights of stairs to a small door, and then reached into the capacious pocket at the front of her starched white apron and produced a small key, which she pressed into Holmes's hand. Then she turned and hurried back down to the ground floor. Holmes turned the key in the lock and we entered Persano's private room. It was small and square, with one window looking down on a backyard, and sparsely furnished. There was a leather-topped desk with a plain chair in front of it, where Persano presumably produced his journalistic efforts, and on the opposite side of the room was a comfortable armchair with a little round table next to it. This was doubtless where he took occasional refreshment and rest from his labours.

The walls were painted a uniform cream and had no pictures on them. The floor was covered only by bare wooden boards, save for a thick round rug which lay under the leg space of the desk. I stood in the doorway and watched as Holmes carried out a very thorough examination. He pulled out his glass and ran it along the sill, the edges, and catches of the window. After covering the floor, he went to the desk and pulled out its three drawers. The second and third contained some sheaves of paper, which he gave only a cursory glance, but a small revolver lay in the first. Holmes opened it up and looked at the chambers, then sniffed the barrel and put it back.

"Well, Watson, I think the study has provided us with all the information it can. Let us return downstairs." On the ground floor once more, Holmes asked Maisie to let us see the backyard. It was a small square space covered in concrete with three walls, about six-and-a-half-feet in height, which separated it from the yards of the houses on either side and of that of the corresponding house in the next street. The back wall of Persano's house was plain, save for a drainpipe about a foot-and-a-half from the window of the study.

"Thank you for your help, Maisie," Holmes said to the maid as she showed us to the door. Once we were back in the street, he turned to me, and, before I could ask what he had learned from the house, said, "You may as well return to Baker Street. I have several more visits to make, and some laborious tasks to perform. But have no fear. I assure you that as my friend and chronicler you will be present at the denouement of this little drama."

He waved his long thin hand in farewell and was gone. It being a warm, sunny morning, I decided to walk back to our lodgings and arrived there to see that the morning papers had been delivered. I sat down to read them, but found the problem of Isidore Persano preying on my mind, so that I had to lay *The Daily Telegraph* aside and give my thought over to it entirely – but I could come up with no solution to the mystery that didn't either rely on some untenable coincidence, or failed to address all the aspects of the case. In the end, I gave up the enterprise and concentrated on the splendid lunch Mrs. Hudson served me at two o'clock. Two hours later, Holmes returned in an excellent mood.

"Well, Watson, I have managed to carry out all my researches successfully."

"And?"

"I will apprise you of the results on our journey to Stoke Newington."

"Where have you been?" I asked.

"Oh, to the shipping office, the Registrar of Births, Marriages and Deaths, the files of *The Daily Star*, Colney Hatch, and West Kensington. But come, I have a hansom waiting for us."

Once in the cab, I was eager to hear what progress Holmes had made in the case.

"Were you able to find out anything about the worm?" I asked as the hansom moved off.

"While the flora and fauna of Africa have yet to be fully categorised, those of South America are even less so. I considered that the balance of probability was that any hitherto unknown species was likely to originate there, and my supposition turned out to be correct. I took the liberty of having the worm examined by Professor George Edward Challenger, who has recently returned to London from one of his expeditions to the Matto Grosso. He recognised it instantly. The creature is indigenous to a very confined region on the banks of the Amazon River. It is the totem animal of the Sigoro Indians. The Professor himself had intended to bring a sample of it to the Royal Society, but it was lost, along with several other interesting specimens, when a pack mule missed its footing and plunged to its death while the expedition was negotiating a narrow cliffside pass."

"Interesting, but how one did come to be in a matchbox on Isidore Persano's desk?"

"Clearly it was placed there by someone who wished Persano no good, since they must have known what kind of reaction it would produce. You will recall that Maisie assured us that no packages had been delivered that day. So either Persano had brought it in himself, which was unlikely, or another person broke in and left it there. When I examined the window, I found signs that it had, indeed, been forced. Persano's study looks out onto the yard and the study is on the third floor. But a young, fit man might have climbed over the walls and up the drainpipe, and done the deed without being observed."

"But why his extreme reaction?"

"I have formulated three possible answers to that question, but I have as yet insufficient data to form a definite conclusion."

"You said you went to the shipping office."

"Yes, to ascertain the most recent arrival times of ships from Rio de Janeiro. Brazil figures largely in this case, and I shall be surprised if we don't discover that Isidore Persano's native language isn't Spanish but Portuguese. It has to be said that the English aren't a race noted for our ability with foreign languages, and the two are easily confused."

"So someone has come from Brazil with the intent of harming Persano."

"So I read it."

My features, which Holmes has often told me are a true mirror of my thoughts, must at that moment have displayed the bafflement I was feeling.

"Why didn't they simply kill him? If they were able to get into his study, why didn't they just wait until he arrived home and went in there, do the deed, and then escape by the way they came?"

"Clearly his immediate death wasn't part of their plan. My apologies, my dear Watson. Again, I have suppositions, but I will not share them with you until they have some substance. Anyway, from the shipping office I went to the Registrar of Births, Marriages, and Deaths, where I made an interesting discovery concerning Dr. Thomas Poulteney: Far from being a bachelor, he has been married for the last seventeen years to one Alice Poulteney, *née* Dawson, of Selsey in the county of West Sussex."

To my mind, Holmes's endeavours seemed to have produced more questions than answers.

"Then why does he represent himself as single, particularly when people are interpreting his friendship with Persano as meaning, well . . . that he is of the 'other persuasion'? And if he really is that way, wouldn't marriage be a way of silencing that sort of gossip?"

"I have no experience of the married state, Watson, as you well know, but I imagine that sort of arrangement wouldn't make for a happy union, whether the spouse knew the truth or not. It would explain his estrangement from his wife, but I'm reasonably sure that Thomas Poulteney isn't, as you so quaintly put it, 'of the other persuasion'. From the Registrar, I went to the offices of *The Daily Star*, where I spent rather longer sifting through the back issues in search of details of his career. It turned out that while he is now most famous as a chemist, he began as an alienist. While researching the composition of certain drugs used in the repression and control of undesirable mental states, he discovered that chemistry was more congenial to him, took a second degree in that subject, and has flourished ever since."

"Are you saying that Persano has always been mad? That his friendship with Poulteney is rather a relationship between a doctor and his patient?"

"No, Watson, that is not what I am saying, though Poulteney's former career certainly has a bearing on the case. But if you have any more questions about Dr. Poulteney, you may ask the man himself, for unless I am mistaken, we have arrived at 17 Margrave Villas, Stoke Newington." The hansom had indeed drawn to a stop even as he spoke.

The house was old and large without being ostentatious, and was surrounded by a small border of greenery with a sturdy iron fence. While I paid the cabbie, Holmes jumped out, opened the gate, bounded along the concrete path, and pulled at the bell. I managed to draw alongside just as the door was opened by a tall and imposing butler with muttonchop whiskers and an air of command.

"Yes?" he said, raising his bushy eyebrows. Holmes produced one of his cards and handed it to the man. "Sherlock Holmes and Dr. John Watson to see Dr. Poulteney."

The butler took the card into his master and returned after a few seconds. "The doctor will see you, gentlemen," he said, and ushered us into Poulteney's receiving room. The man sitting behind the desk was in his mid-forties, his thick wavy black hair and beard streaked with grey, but still remarkably trim and handsome. As he rose to greet us, it could be seen that he was a little under the average height, but this slight lack of stature did nothing to diminish the aura of power and intelligence that hung around him like a cloak.

"That will be all, Hanson. You may go."

"Hanson," said Holmes as the servant turned to the door, "you were a sergeant-major."

"Yes, sir."

"In the infantry."

"Yes sir, 13th Regiment."

"Hanson?"

"Begging your pardon, sir. Good day, gentlemen."

"Clearly a non-commissioned officer, but too heavy to be a sapper or a lancer," said Holmes after the butler had closed the door behind him.

"Mr. Holmes," Poulteney began, "I have heard a little of your reputation. I take it you haven't come to my house merely to demonstrate your ability at parlour tricks."

Holmes gave a little smile. "I do apologise, Dr. Poulteney. The exercise of the faculty of logical deduction can become a little addictive. No, we are here to ask you some questions about the disappearance of your friend, Mr. Isidore Persano."

"I gave all the information I have to the police yesterday, but I have no objection to giving it again if you think it will be of value."

"I think that it will, Dr. Poulteney, but let me first say that, unlike the detectives of the official force, I am a free agent, and therefore not restrained by professional delicacy. I trust you understand me."

"Completely. Ask me whatever you like. I have nothing to hide."

"Very well," said Holmes, leaning back slightly in his chair and crossing his ankles. "Firstly, can you tell us exactly where and when you first met Mr. Persano?"

"It was something like three years ago. I was invited to a literary dinner by a mutual friend and Mr. Persano was also present."

"And did you hit it off straight away? How did you become friends?"

"Well, he certainly struck me as a charming and erudite individual, but as to when I began to truly consider him a friend, who can say? How does someone cease to be merely an acquaintance and become a friend?"

"Would you say that Mr. Persano is your best friend?"

"Yes, yes I would."

"Then I must say I am rather surprised at the lack of concern you appear to be showing at his disappearance."

"I am not the kind of person who puts his emotions on display, but I assure you, I am deeply disturbed by this event, or I wouldn't have agreed to answer your questions. Though I must say, I doubt the relevance of what you have asked me so far. And now, if you don't mind, I generally have a cup of tea at this time. Will you join me?"

"Why not?" said Holmes. Poulteney tugged at the bell pull, and a minute later the door behind us opened and a maid brought in a tray. I caught no more than a glimpse of her slim back and a loose black braid of hair surmounted by a little white cap, and then she was gone. "And now," resumed Holmes after a sip of tea, "I must ask you a question which will seem the height of impertinence to you, but which must be asked if I am to penetrate to the heart of this case."

"Then ask, sir," said Poulteney calmly.

"Were the relations between you and *Señor* Isidore Persano . . . *abnormal* in any way?"

"I can promise you," Poulteney said with a steady voice, "that our 'relations', as you call them, were in no manner what could be termed unnatural. Nor has there been any impropriety, of any kind, between us."

"Such was my belief," said Holmes, "but I was bound to ask. Do you know anything of Mr. Persano's life before he came to London?"

"I was aware that he had lived in Paris, but I know nothing of his life before that."

"And do you have any inkling of his present whereabouts?"

"None whatever. If I had, I would of course have informed the police."

"Dear me, Dr. Poulteney," said Holmes, shaking his head in mock sorrow, "for the most part, you have, with some difficulty, stayed broadly within the bounds of truth, but your last two statements were outright lies."

Dr. Poulteney rose to his feet, his face white with anger. "How dare you, sir! I must ask you and your colleague to leave my house this instant!"

"Sit down, Doctor," said Holmes imperturbably. "Allow me to assure you that my sympathies in this matter are entirely on your side, and that the best possible outcome will be achieved by your complete cooperation." The chemist resumed his seat, but his expression was tense and wary. "I shall reconstruct the situation as I understand it, and you may correct me whenever my deductions diverge from the strict truth," continued Holmes.

Dr. Poulteney nodded. "Very well."

"On the evening in question, you received an urgent message from *Señor* Persano's maidservant, informing you that her master had been taken to the asylum at Colney Hatch. You immediately put a set of women's clothing and a long wig in a valise and hurried by carriage to the asylum. There you had no difficulty obtaining entry, for this was the place where you had been a resident immediately before your change in profession, and your face was still well known. You had either retained a set of keys, or knew where in the building a set could be easily obtained. You also knew the location of the holding cells where a new patient was likely to be brought. You waited until an orderly had checked on *Señor* Persano and, being aware of the asylum's routine, you knew how long it would be before he or she returned.

"You opened the cell door, stripped Persano of his male attire, and dressed him in the woman's outfit. Doubtless you put his clothing in the valise, since it wasn't found in the room when his disappearance was discovered. I don't know if Persano was conscious or not by this time, but in any event, it would have been easy to take him to another cell until he awoke. Then you waited until a new security shift came on, and you and Persano were allowed through the gates. The new guards recognised you but didn't know that you had entered the asylum on your own. They had no reason to assume that the woman accompanying you was an inmate. And so you and Persano made your escape."

"I had kept my keys from the time of my residency," said Poulteney. "I found Isidore asleep, and yes, I carried him to another cell. But after he awoke, I allowed him to change his clothes himself while I kept my back turned. Otherwise, your deductions are correct. However, for all your cleverness, sir, there is one crucial aspect you haven't uncovered."

"Oh, I have uncovered it, Dr. Poulteney, I merely haven't mentioned it yet. Watson here can tell you that I have a lamentable predilection for the dramatic." So saying, he leaned forward and gave the bell pull a sharp jerk. Moments later the maid reappeared, her head modestly bowed, and moved to take the tray. As she bent to do so, Holmes seized her cap and hair and pulled them off, revealing a closely cropped head. "Watson, allow me to introduce Isidore – I beg her pardon – I should say, *Miss Isadora* Persano." For while her face might have passed for that of a handsome young man, her form, though slim, was unmistakably female.

Dr. Thomas Poulteney instantly stood and enfolded her in a protective embrace. "It began as friendship," he said in a gentle tone, "but it blossomed into something deeper. Then one day Isadora revealed her secret to me, and I realised we were in love. But there was a reason why I couldn't ask her to be my wife."

"You were already married – to Alice Dawson."

"Yes, and I rue the day that ever I stood beside her at the altar. She had deceived me into completely misreading her character, and no sooner was the ring on her finger than she embarked on a series of adulterous affairs. She drank, and experimented with stimulants of various kinds. It became obvious to me that while there had as yet been no public scandal, it was only a matter of time. Finally, I reached an agreement with her that she should move out of my house. I provided her with a monthly allowance on the condition that she lived under another name and made no further demands on me. My existing friends knew of this arrangement and kept my secret, so that when I made new acquaintances, I was thus able to represent myself as a bachelor. Although in the course of my social life I met many women, I had hardened my heart against the emotion of love. And then I met Isadora." As he said this, he took the young woman's hand in his own. Both smiled, and they gazed into each other's eyes with such clear affection that I felt a wave of warmth and sympathy towards them.

"And now, Miss Persano," said Holmes, "I believe the time has come for you to give us an explanation of those points which we haven't already resolved."

"Very well, Mr. Holmes," she began in a low, melodious voice. She lowered her eyes, and when she raised them a few seconds later they were full of frankness and resolution.

"I was born on the banks of the Imara, a river which runs into the Amazon some five hundred miles from its source. My father was a Portuguese missionary named Dr. Jorge Persano, and my mother was a member of the Sigoro Indian tribe which inhabits that region. My father converted many of the tribesmen and women to Christianity – including of course my mother – but the majority of them continued to adhere to the cult of Tumaq, a god whom they worshipped in the form of the worm that appeared in my study. For some years this was of no matter. My father also ran a school, and all were encouraged to make use of it, whatever their religious persuasion. But the time came when the followers of Christ began to outnumber those of Tumaq, and the priests began to mutter that my father should be expelled, and those he had converted forcibly returned to their original creed.

"Sensing the danger, my father formulated plans to send me to Manaus to ensure my safety, but before this could be done, there was an uprising. My parents were killed, and the worship of Tumaq restored. I was then nine years old. It was decided that when I attained womanhood, I was to be a 'Bride of Tumaq', which meant that I would be sacrificed to the god at the summer solstice following my first menstruation. Until that day arrived I would be a prisoner, although I would be clothed in the finest fabrics and given the choicest foods. I lived in dread of the day when I would first experience my monthly courses, but before that evil hour arrived, I was spirited away by a small group who still secretly adhered to Christ, and taken to Manaus as my father had originally planned. There I sought out the Archbishop, who was an old friend of my father and grieved much to hear of his fate. He raised me in his house and saw that I was educated.

"I turned sixteen, and thought that my previous unhappy experiences were well behind me, but I discovered, to my sorrow, that I was wrong. I mentioned that my father had run a school in the Sigoro village. He had unwittingly nurtured a group of young men who could speak Spanish, Portuguese, and English, but remained fanatical devotees of the Worm God. When they heard of my escape, they swore that, if it meant going to the ends of the earth, they would capture me and take me back to become a Bride of Tumaq, for if one who had been promised to him didn't meet her fate at the designated time, the whole tribe would suffer for it until the situation was rectified. An attempt was made to kidnap me in Manaus, but it was thwarted, and one of the offenders captured by the police, and it was he who warned me that, go where I would, the followers of Tumaq would track me down.

"I determined that I would go to Europe, and the good Archbishop readily gave me the wherewithal. I arrived in Paris, where I first cut off my long hair and assumed men's clothing. As further protection, I carried a gun and learned how to use it well. My education enabled me to obtain work as a journalist, but I was young, and unwise enough to write an article criticising an eminent businessman and accusing him of corrupt practices. He challenged me to a duel in the cemetery at Pere Lachaise, and I killed him. Both his sons then challenged me, and met the same fate as their father. I thus acquired a reputation as a duellist, though I had challenged no one. I was unhappy with this, so I quit Paris and came to London. It was here, as you have heard, that I first met Thomas, and when an intimate friendship began to turn into love, I revealed my true sex to him.

"Because of the English divorce laws, we couldn't marry, but we spent as much time together as possible. A fellow journalist named Marlowe made sly accusations. I lost my temper and challenged him to a duel. Later, we took adjoining rooms at a hotel run by Arnold Campbell when we holidayed in Brighton together. He also accused my darling of having a perverted passion. For myself I didn't care, but these men were impugning the honour of the best man who ever drew breath. I couldn't let such insults pass. I challenged Campbell too, and in both cases I was careful to merely wound them. Honour was satisfied. As to the Sigoro totem, I confess that when I came home that evening and found that despicable worm on my desk. I succumbed to hysteria.

"Do you wonder at that, Mr. Holmes? Dr. Watson? Since the age of nine this thing had been a symbol of horror in my life, and now at the age of thirty, when I believed that I was more or less safe, and felt secure in the love of the best of men, this abomination was back to haunt me. I understood only too clearly the message its presence sent: That the followers of Tumaq had managed to pursue me to London, that they would capture me and take me back to the banks of the Imara to die at the next summer solstice. I suppose that by taunting me thus, they hoped to frighten me so badly that I would be rendered incapable of clear thought or action. The rest I think you know."

At Holmes's instructions, the police made a thorough and painstaking list of all those who had come into London from Brazil in the last two months, and by a process of elimination and identification, assisted by Miss Persano, they were able to arrest the handful of men from the Sigoro tribe who had threatened her life. All suffered permanent deportation. For the first time in her life, Isadora felt completely free.

We were back in Baker Street a few days later, enjoying a pipe after our evening meal, when I turned to Holmes and said, "There's one thing I don't understand. I almost got the feeling that Poulteney wanted us to find out the truth. Why else did he ring for Isadora to bring the tea?"

"Well, Dr. Poulteney isn't a criminal, but in this respect he shares one of their characteristics: That when an imposture has been carried off successfully, the perpetrator has an unspoken desire for it to be discovered, so that everyone may see and admire his cleverness."

"That is surely rather fanciful."

"Is it? Well, if that doesn't serve your turn, consider this: Here we have two people who for almost three years have been forced to conceal their true relationship and unable to openly express the deep love they feel for each other. Imagine how great a relief it must be to finally be able to openly acknowledge those feelings, even if there is still an element of danger in the revelation."

"That, I suspect, is closer to the truth."

"And is, no doubt, the version you will give your readers."

"No, Holmes. I may make a record of this case, but I hardly think it can be published in our lifetimes. It contains certain themes, certain references . . . ."

"Ah, to what Lord Alfred Douglas called 'the love that dare not speak its name'. But there was no true instance of such a love here. It was all in the minds of a few individuals."

"Even so, I suspect that the public wouldn't wish to hear of it. Perhaps one day . . . ."

"Yes, let us hope so."

Little more remains to be said. Thomas Poulteney and Isadora continued to remain in their celibate state for another year or so, when they received news that Poulteney's estranged wife, Alice, had been killed in a boating accident, freeing them to marry. Thomas received a knighthood for his services to science in 1905. He and Lady Poulteney became well-known members of high society, to say nothing of producing three beautiful, olive-skinned children. "Isidore Persano" was never heard of again.

A Yuletide Mystery

Elsewhere in these memoirs, I have stated that of all the cases in which I acted as the companion and amanuensis of my distinguished friend, Mr. Sherlock Holmes, there were only two which I brought to his notice: That of Colonel Warburton's madness, and that of Victor Hatherley and his missing thumb. Since the publication of that story, however, I have had occasion to draw his attention to one other, which the newspapers at the time dubbed "The Yuletide Mystery", as it took place towards the end of a dark and snowbound December.

The King's Road, Chelsea, was crowded with shoppers on that winter afternoon, as I made my way determinedly through the thick snow towards a particular little shop that sold old, second-hand, and obscure books. I was warmly dressed in a thick coat over a tweed suit, a woolen muffler, stout boots, and leather gloves, with a cloth cap covering my head, but a chill, cutting wind was swirling the heavy snowflakes along the busy street, and I would be happy to be back in front of the fire in our rooms in Baker Street.

The bell rang as I stepped inside old Mr. Penfold's shop and pulled off my gloves. The interior felt pleasantly warm, and smelt reassuringly of leather-bound volumes and old ink. Mr. Penfold stepped out of his back room and gazed at me over his half-moon spectacles.

"Dr. Watson! Hello! I haven't seen you or Mr. Holmes in here for some time."

I smiled. With the fluffy little ring of whitening hair about the back of his head, his old-fashioned fingerless gloves, and his embroidered waistcoat, there was something distinctly Dickensian about the old bookseller. He might have stepped from the pages of *The Pickwick Papers* or *Martin Chuzzlewit*.

"I'm here to buy Mr. Holmes a Christmas present," I said. "Do you have any suggestions?"

"Well," said Mr. Penfold, "I've just had a delivery of a complete library. You know, relatives selling off the property of the deceased. I haven't had time to take them out and look at them. Perhaps you'd like to go through it with me, see if anything takes your fancy."

"I'd like that very much."

"Splendid! The crates are just inside the back door. The delivery man was in a hurry, so we just made sure they were out of the cold. Let me get the first one into the office."

"Let me do it, Mr. Penfold. They must be heavy."

"All right, let's do it together."

We pulled the crate next to the desk in the bookseller's office, where a coal fire was glowing in the hearth. Mr. Penfold sat in his wooden chair, leaving me to occupy the rather more comfortable armchair opposite. I took off my hat and coat and sat down.

"Right," he said. "I suggest I take them out first and hand them to you. If it isn't clear what a volume is, I have a better chance of identifying it than you. Oh, while I think of it, would you like a cup of tea? Sorting through books can be dry work."

"I'll do it. That will give you a chance to start going through them."

"Very well. The kitchen is just through there. You can see where everything is."

I was pouring boiling water into a big brown ceramic teapot when Mr. Penfold cried, "Ah, I think I've found something Mr. Holmes would like."

"Oh, what's that?"

"*The Course of Positive Philosophy*, by Auguste Comte."

I put the pot, two cups, the milk jug and the sugar bowl on a tin tray and carried them into the little office.

"I'm afraid he already has it," I said as I laid the tray on the table. I had made a thorough survey of Holmes's bookshelf before coming out.

"Harrison Ainsworth – *The Tower of London* and *Rookwood* and *The Lancashire Witches*. Sir Walter Scott's *Kenilworth*, *Peveril of the Peak*, *Rob Roy*, and *Redgauntlet*. Old Mr. Greville seems to have had quite a taste for historicals. Ah, what about this? *The Mystery of a Hansom Cab*, by Fergus Hume. "

I couldn't help smiling.

"Mr. Holmes has very little patience with the detectives of fiction. None of them seem to come up to his intellectual standards."

"Well, it was quite a big seller a few years ago, I seem to recall."

"That would cut no ice with him. 'What does the general public know?' he'd say. 'They cannot even tell a shoemaker by the state of his trousers or a journalist by the condition of his second finger, so how can they be trusted when it comes to evaluating the plausibility of an invented crime investigation?'"

Just then the bell rang. As Mr. Penfold rose to go into the shop, he said. "Carry on looking. I shouldn't be too long."

There was nothing Holmes would have cared to read in the rest of that crate, so I went to the back door, made a pile of about twelve books from the second crate and carried them into the office. I put the pile on the floor next to the armchair and picked up the first volume. It was a copy of Kipling's first collection of short stories, *Plain Tales from the Hills*. Now, the reader might imagine that given my experiences in our Eastern possessions, the wounds I had sustained during the Afghan campaign, and my subsequent bout with enteric fever, I would have no desire to revisit those dark days, even via the medium of fiction. It is a curious fact, but with the passage of time, what remained with me was the memory, not of my pains, but of the stout fellows I had met and befriended, and of the courage and self-sacrifice they had shown. I set the Kipling volume to one side for myself.

The next two books in the pile were distinctly promising – a collection of the poems of Francois Villon in French – Holmes disdained translations if he had a grasp of the original language – and a book on fingerprints by Sir Francis Galton.

I could hear Mr. Penfold finishing up with his latest customer.

"Right, sir. So, the complete Galland *Thousand and One Nights*, Sir Richard Burton's *The Gold Mines of Midian*, and *The Episodes of Vathek* by William Beckford. Not many of that last one about. Nice edition, too. That'll be twenty-five pounds, thank you sir. And a good Christmas to you too, sir."

I placed my empty cup in its saucer, put on my cap and coat, and went out into the shop, handed Mr. Penfold the little pile and reached into my pocket for my wallet.

"I've found three things I'd like. How much is that?"

"Six pounds, please."

I pulled out the exact amount and Mr. Penfold wrote me a receipt.

"Would you like these delivered?"

"No, I'll take them now."

"Oh, in that case I'll wrap them up and put them in a bag for you. Don't want the snow getting at them, do we? Now, where did I put that brown paper?"

He turned to a shelf behind him.

The bell rang, and there was a brief gust of cold air as the door was opened and closed. Mr. Penfold turned around. The shop was empty.

Sherlock Holmes took a sip from his hot toddy and leaned forward eagerly in his armchair.

"Ah, at last, Watson, you come to the nub of the matter! Why did you leave old Mr. Penfold's shop in so precipitous a manner? You had seen something, I take it, but what?"

"I saw a murder, Holmes. What made me glance through the window of the bookshop at precisely that moment I cannot say. It was already dark and snowy, but there was a streetlamp nearby. The victim was leaning up against the lamppost, and the other man – the killer – was very close, right in front of him. I saw something glitter in his hand, and then he thrust upward, up through the ribcage into the heart. The victim must have died instantaneously. Then the murderer pulled the knife out, put it in his pocket and left his victim propped against the post."

"And no else saw the killing take place?"

"Apparently not. As I said, it was dark, and snowing heavily. After a second's hesitation I decided that I had to pursue the killer, as there was nothing I could do for the victim. At that moment, a tram pulled up at a nearby stop, and the culprit jumped on board. As it pulled away, I was forced to run after it, fearing all the time that I would lose my footing and tumble forward onto the icy road. But I managed to reach it and pull myself up onto the platform."

"Well done. That was no small feat for a middle-aged man with a damaged *tendo Achillis*."

"I was in time to see him climbing the stairs to the upper deck, so I took a seat on the lower deck and waited for him to come down. When the conductor asked me for my fare, I had to buy a ticket for the terminus at Highbury, as I had no idea where my quarry would be getting off. Eventually he descended at The Angel, Islington. His face, as before, was half-obscured by a woolen scarf, but I had no doubt as to his identity. I had also seen that the collar of his overcoat had a distinctive red trimming."

"Excellent, old friend! Your powers of observation certainly seem to be improving. What happened then?"

"He crossed the road and I followed him, at a distance, through a maze of very similar streets, until he entered a house. Number 43. I went to the end of the road and made a note of its name, Allingham Street. As you know, I do not have your encyclopedic knowledge of the metropolis, so I found myself wandering those near-identical streets, trying to find a way back to the Pentonville Road."

"Where you knew there was a police station, from one of our previous exploits in that area."

"Quite so. I was lucky enough to encounter a beat officer who escorted me to the station, where I made a full statement of what I had seen and how I had followed the fellow to his house. I don't doubt that I will be called upon to testify when the case comes to trial."

"A fine afternoon's work, dear doctor. And now, I am sure you are more than ready for one of Mrs. Hudson's splendid suppers."

The following morning, the papers were full of the King's Road murder. The condition of the victim, whose identity remained as yet unknown, was not discovered until a passerby bumped into him, and his corpse was knocked to the snowy ground, where it left conspicuous red stains. As of the next day, the Metropolitan Police stated they were confident that an early arrest would be made, as they had already received vital evidence from an eye witness, whose name they declined to reveal in the interests of that individual's personal security.

I imagined that the matter was settled, and that there was no more to be done until I was summoned to appear before the court. When the early edition of *The Evening Standard* arrived, however, it told a different story. The Christmas murder, as they were calling it, the 25th being only a few days away, was still unsolved. The suspect, when questioned by the police, pointed out by the still-unnamed eye-witness had an unshakeable alibi, having been with his sister and brother at the time in question.

"Hardly what I'd call unshakeable," said Holmes after I had drawn the article to his attention. "I'm sure the Scotland Yard files are bursting with cases where a spouse or a sibling, or a parent, has lied to support a murderer. Does it mention anywhere who is in charge of the investigation? I can't imagine Bradstreet, or Gregson, or even Lestrade making such a cardinal mistake."

I glanced further down the article until I reached the name.

"Inspector Drayton."

"No, I don't know him. He must be a recent addition, or elevation, to the ranks of the detective division."

"Holmes, it's always possible that I followed the wrong man. That is the conclusion most people would come to. It was dark, and the snow was heavy."

"If I had to cite every instance of 'the conclusion most people would come to' being utterly and demonstrably wrong, we'd be here 'til tomorrow morning."

My old friend reached forward and patted me reassuringly on the arm.

"As so often, your characteristic modesty leads you to underestimate your own abilities. I have no doubt that the man you pursued was the culprit, as I am sure our investigations will confirm."

"Our investigations? You intend to look into the matter?"

"I can hardly see how I could do otherwise, so let us begin. You said the killer put the murder weapon straight in his pocket?"

"Yes."

"So, Inspector Drayton should have had the pockets examined for bloodstains. On the basis of what we know so far, that gentleman doesn't seem fated to rise any higher in the force."

"Perhaps not, but what should we do?"

"We find out the name of the man, and as much as we can about him. It would help if we can discover the identity of the victim, too. It's unusual for someone to have no form of identification on him at all, not even a wallet."

"Should we call on Inspector Drayton and ask him about the suspect?"

"As far as Scotland Yard is concerned the fellow's been cleared, so he will not be permitted to give us that information. But we have the man's address, so it will only require a visit to the Town Clerk for Islington and an examination of the electoral roll to provide us with his name. No, stay where you are, Watson, and remain by the fire. This task only requires one of us."

He stood, took his heavy coat from its hook, and went to the door.

The Islington electoral register revealed that the inhabitants of 43 Allingham Street (or at least, those eligible to vote) were two men, Jonathan and Christopher Morton.

"Our next move," said Holmes, "must be to ascertain what employment the man has, if any. We will keep the house under surveillance, and when he comes out, I will follow him, while you continue to watch the house. That will mean getting there early in the morning, before most people are up, so I suggest that you get a good night's sleep."

"Holmes, the fellow is a murderer. Should we not both follow him? What if he should turn on you?"

"Your concern is touching, Watson, but a little misplaced. However bulky and formidable the man may be, I have my knowledge of the Eastern martial arts, and I am confident that I can hold my own in any confrontation."

"Nevertheless, he may be armed. I will take my revolver, and I urge you to do the same."

"Very well, if it will ease your mind."

Perhaps my awareness of the importance and potential danger of our task was colouring my perceptions, but my memory of the following morning is that it was the darkest and coldest of the year. Even as we made our way through the pre-dawn streets in a hansom cab which Holmes had ordered the previous evening, the snow was descending in great sheets which were then scattered and dispersed by the icy swirling winds. Looking through the cab window, it was almost as if we were inside one of those glass snow globes, and in my imagination a giant hand might at any moment shake the globe and plunge us into a hazy white chaos where up was down and back was front.

At last we arrived at No. 43 Allingham Street. Holmes paid the cab fare, and I wished the driver a Merry Christmas. Then we alighted and began to look around for a suitable location from which we might observe the door of the murderer's dwelling. By great good fortune, a house which was almost opposite No. 43 was derelict and unoccupied. Holmes glanced briefly around to make sure that we were unobserved, then plied his lock-pick, and within moments we were inside. Through the windows of the front parlour, we had a clear view of the killer's door.

We didn't have long to wait. At about half-past-six, the man himself came out of the house.

"That's him," I whispered.

"You're sure?"

"Same height, same coat, same hat."

Holmes waited a few seconds, then made for the front door. I followed, and gripped his arm for a second.

"Be careful."

Holmes said nothing, but smiled at me, and then he was gone.

He returned to the empty house at about half-past-two in the afternoon. We walked to Pentonville Road, where we found a cab to take us home. On the journey back to Baker Street, we said little. I was waiting to return to the warmth and comfort of our rooms before sharing my experience, while Holmes appeared to be contemplating what he had seen and sifting through it for what was relevant and what might be discarded. A fire was blazing in the sitting room grate when we arrived at No. 221b, and as we took our seats, our landlady brought in a plate piled high with sandwiches and laid it on the table between us.

"You went out early without any breakfast," she said, "so I thought you might be hungry. I didn't make anything hot, because I didn't know what time you'd be back."

"And you lit the fire too," I said, reaching for a cheese-and-tomato sandwich. "Mrs. Hudson, you are an absolute angel."

"Well, I don't know about that. Would you like some coffee?"

"An excellent idea," said Holmes. "Just the antidote to a short night's sleep and several long hours spent out in the cold."

When most of the sandwiches had been consumed and the coffee cups were empty, I looked across at Holmes.

"I have little doubt that your morning was more interesting than mine,"I said, "so I'm eager to hear about it."

Holmes reached into the coal scuttle for his cigars and we each took one from the box. When they were both lit and drawing well, he began.

"Our friend caught a tram from the Angel, and I just managed to get on it. He alighted at Bank Station and walked to what I imagine must be his place of work, a law firm called Stringer and Cunliffe in Mercer's Lane. Judging from where he lives, he cannot be a solicitor, so he must be something like a clerk. If he was a messenger, he would have gone out, and I would have seen him, as I was seated on a little bench opposite the building. Anyway, he left at about quarter-past-twelve, and I followed him to a cafe where I assume he was having his lunch, and I came back to you. When exactly did you see him outside the shop?"

"At about half-past four."

"He started work at seven-thirty, so I wouldn't have thought he'd be out until four at the earliest. Bank to King's Road, Chelsea. That's an eleven tram. With the traffic at that time, in this sort of weather, it's unlikely he'd be there by half-past four."

"He might have had the afternoon off. Some companies do that at Christmas so their employees can go shopping for presents. Or perhaps he doesn't start at the same time every day."

"Possibly, though neither of those things usually apply to law firms. What did you see?"

"The only person who called, at a quarter-to-ten, was a tradesman of some sort, and I caught a glimpse of a wife, or sister or whatever she might be, when she answered the door to him. I didn't see anyone else."

Holmes stood up.

"I have to go out again."

"Whatever for?"

"I have to buy an overcoat."

"I can't see that there's anything wrong with the one you have."

"Nor is there. I should be back in time for dinner."

When he returned at about half-past-six, he was carrying a parcel wrapped in brown paper which I assumed contained his new overcoat. As we ate our evening meal, he made it clear that he didn't wish to discuss the case. After our long association, I was used to this reticence on his part, nor did it come as any surprise to me when, the following morning, he steered our conversation over breakfast onto trivial and commonplace lines. I knew that when he saw fit, he would give me a full account of his doings, whatever they might be. He left at about half-past-eleven, wearing his new purchase, and returned at about two. After taking a light lunch, he lit a cigarette and embarked on an explanation.

"Human beings, as you know, are creatures of habit, so my purchase of an overcoat similar to that of Mr. Morton was predicated on the belief that he would lunch at the same cafe as he had the previous day. When a man finds an establishment to his liking within a few minutes' walk of his place of work, he is likely to return to it. And so it proved. The cafe, which was in South Place, E.C., was fairly crowded, but fortunately there were one or two empty places. I watched through the front window as he hung up his coat. He then went over to the counter to order his lunch and sat down opposite another diner to wait for the arrival of his food. I went in, took off my coat and hung it on the hook next to his. I ordered and paid for a cup of tea and found a sear near the window. When my tea arrived, I drank it at a leisurely pace, after which I left, making sure to lift Morton's overcoat from its hook instead of my own."

"You wished to examine it, and using this subterfuge, you could claim that you had taken it by mistake if he challenged you on it."

"Exactly. A swift glance in his direction as I went through the door told me that he was only halfway through his meal. I went a few yards down the street and turned a corner. Then I took off the coat and looked at the pockets, where I found his wallet, which identified him as *Jonathan*, rather than *Christopher* Morton. Fortunately that style of overcoat has pockets you can pull out and examine. In the other there was a distinct bloodstain, which by its colour seemed to be fairly recent. When I returned to the cafe Morton was just finishing his first course and was about to start on a bowl of apple pie and cream. I put his coat back on the hook, donned my own, and made my exit. Then I went to Scotland Yard to tell them what I'd found. There was a little bit of a stink – Drayton was in charge of the case, but Gregson was there too, and as the senior man, he had some harsh words for Drayton for not having had Morton's clothing examined the first time they brought him in. Anyway, speaking of coats, get yours."

"Why?"

"They're bringing Morton in, and Gregson convinced Drayton that we should be there."

42

By the time we arrived at the station, there had been fresh developments. The corpse had been identified as Michael Byrne of 22 Arlington Road, Peckham.

"You took the afternoon off from Stringer and Cunliffe because you said there was a family emergency and you needed to get back to Islington," Drayton, a big young man with a head of frizzy red hair, was saying to Morton as we came into the interrogation room with Inspector Gregson. "What was the nature of this 'family emergency'?"

"None of your damn business."

"Since your presence at 43 Allingham Road constitutes your alibi, I'd say it's very much 'our business'. You weren't at Allingham Road, were you? You were in King's Road, Chelsea, at approximately four-thirty, stabbing Michael Byrne to death. Then you went back to Islington and convinced your brother and sister to tell us you'd been there since you got back from work. Isn't that what really happened?"

There was a knock at the door. It was opened to reveal the station sergeant, accompanied by a young man, who, to judge from the similarity of their features and their blond hair, could only be Morton's brother.

"This is Mr. Christopher Morton," said the sergeant, "and he says he has information vital to this case."

The other brother half rose from his seat and cried, "No, Chris, no!" before he was pushed back into his chair by Drayton.

"I'm sorry, Jon, but the truth must be told. This business has gone far enough."

"What about what we swore to mother? What about the lambs?"

"Curse the bloody lambs! You've given up the best years of your life, and for what? So that this could happen?"

"Why are you here, Chris? And what have you done with her?"

"I gave her a pill and locked her in her room. She'll be out for hours."

"I think it would help," said Gregson. "If you could tell us what this is all about . . . ."

"On the morning of the murder, Jonathan thought the weather was going to be a little warmer, so he left his heavier topcoat at home and put on a lighter one – "

"Chris, don't do this!"

"Our sister Alice is Jon's twin. They're the same height, and Alice is quite broad-shouldered for a woman. Alice has had mental problems for quite a long time – "

"Oh God!" said Jonathan, and covered his face with his hands.

"But when mother was dying, Jon promised that he'd always look after her – that we'd both always look after her. And as long as one of us was there, she was usually all right. Jon is better with her than I am, but we needed money, and as he is also a better earner than I am, he worked and I stayed home with Alice. But lately, she's been getting more difficult to handle, and we started giving her drugs. I suppose whatever they did to her, she blamed it on me. I was about to give her that morning's medication. I turned my back on her for one moment, and the next thing I knew, she hit me on the back of my head with something, and I came around at about two. She'd taken Jonathan's overcoat, one of my hats, and a sharp knife we use for cutting vegetables. I got one of the boys on our street to take a message to Jon to summon him home. When he arrived, there was nothing we could do but wait. Alice came in and we feared the worst. We knew she could be violent because – because – "

"No, Chris, no. Please."

"We knew she could be violent because my mother died because Alice stabbed her. Our doctor was an old family friend. He falsified the death certificate to say she died of heart failure."

"You should have put her in an institution," said Drayton. "They would have known how to deal with her there."

Jonathan turned to the inspector, his eyes blazing with anger.

"Have you ever seen the inside of one of those places? Well, have you? If you had, you'd never, ever think of putting someone you loved in there."

"I'm afraid the price paid for your reluctance to do so was the life of an innocent man," said Holmes, "killed at random by the sound of it."

Christopher resumed his narrative.

"She came home at about six, in a state of exhaustion, not knowing where she'd been, or what she'd been doing. We put her to bed, and I found the bloody knife in one pocket and this in the other."

He tossed a brown leather wallet on the table. The letters "*MB*" were embossed on one corner.

"That doesn't tell in her favour," said Gregson. "It makes it look as if a robbery was a motive. But from what you have told us, she may well be found irresponsible due to insanity. As for you gentlemen, I'm afraid the penalties for being accessories after the fact can be severe, whatever the judge decides about your sister's culpability. We must arrest you. Take them to the cells, Sergeant, and then arrange for their sister to be brought here."

"We weren't like the lambs after all, were we?" said Jonathan.

"No, we weren't," his brother replied.

After the Morton brothers had been taken to the cells. Drayton said, "So what the Hell was all that business about '*lambs*'? What have bloody sheep got to do with any of it?"

"It wasn't '*lambs*' with a small '*l*'," said Holmes. "It was '*Lambs*' – the name – with a capital '*L*'. Charles and Mary Lamb. They were part of a literary circle that included William Hazlitt and Samuel Taylor Coleridge, and wrote a book for children together called *Tales from Shakespeare*."

"I'm no wiser," said Drayton.

"Well, they were brother and sister. In 1796, Mary suffered a mental breakdown and stabbed her mother to death. She was put in an asylum, but in 1799, Charles took sole charge of her and they began living together in London. As long as she was with

46

Charles, she was balanced and sane. Charles devoted the rest of his life to her and they both died unmarried. Do you understand it now?"

"Pardon me," said Drayton. "I didn't have the benefit of a university education."

"I doubt that the Mortons did either," I said. "Some families read, some don't."

"A sad story all round," I remarked to Holmes the following evening. "Poor Michael Byrne killed, Alice Morton likely to spend the rest of her life in an institution, separated from her brothers, and the pair of them doomed to serve whatever term in prison the judge deems fit."

"We cannot always hope for a happy ending, Watson, as you well know, and I'm sure you will agree that it is better for all concerned that there should be no chance of Miss Morton roaming the streets with murderous intent, even if she cannot be held responsible. As for her brothers, they may come before a sympathetic judge."

"Or they may not."

"Come, old friend, tomorrow is Christmas, one of your favourite times of the year, and I happen to know that Mrs. Hudson has made a special effort this Yuletide. I don't believe I've ever seen so large and plump a goose."

Christmas! In all the flurry and activity of the previous few days, I had completely forgotten the books I had purchased at Mr. Penfold's shop.

There was a ring at the door. Mrs. Hudson answered and a few moments later a dapper elderly man appeared on our threshold bearing a brown paper parcel. I failed to recognise him at first, but then I knew him.

"Mr. Penfold!"

"I'll only stay a moment. I'm just bringing these around."

He handed over the parcel.

"I'm sorry I didn't bring them earlier, but you know, I close quite late, and I live in the opposite direction. Tonight I'm on my way to spend Christmas with my daughter Susan and her family in Camden Town, so you're on my route,"

"We were just about to have some mulled wine," said Holmes. "Stay and have one with us. Something to warm you up before you go back out into the cold."

"Oh, don't mind if I do. Just the one, though."

"Thank you again, Mr. Penfold," I said, "and Happy Christmas to you."

"And to you, gentlemen. And to you."

The Adventure of the
Silver Snail

Mr. Sherlock Holmes and I were seated at the dining table in our sitting room at 221b Baker Street, smoking an after-breakfast pipe and perusing the morning newspapers, when Holmes gave vent to a short, barking laugh. I looked across at him questioningly. He folded his paper and proffered it to me, tapping the relevant section with the mouthpiece of his pipe.

"As a literary practitioner, dear Doctor, what do you make of that?"

I put down *The Telegraph*, took *The Courier* from him, and looked at the article. It read:

At the Supper Table
A weekly column by
The Daily Courier *'s restaurant critic*
Raymond Arnoux

Those of you who are gracious enough to peruse my little essays each week will know that I am not a man to mince my words. I state my conclusions in no uncertain terms. Indeed, how could it be otherwise, when it is my duty to act as a culinary advance guard, braving restaurants where the foot of cultured man has never before trod, and to bring back accurate reports of the wonders, or horrors, that I find there. If, therefore, my conclusions as set out in the following paragraphs seem harsh and acerbic, you may nevertheless rest assured that the establishment in question deserves every iota of the opprobrium I heap upon it.

Like many, I was full of anticipation when I learned that a new French restaurant, L'Auberge de Jehan Cottard, was due to open at 17 Moulton St, Fitzrovia, W. In accordance with my usual policy, I allowed the new enterprise a grace period of two weeks before visiting its premises for the purposes of assessing its value as a venue for the consumption of comestibles worthy of the sophisticated palate. It cannot be gainsaid that the proprietors have made a conspicuous effort to ensure that the decor and ambience are redolent of Magny's or Le Grand Vefour. The waiters are modest, efficient, and inconspicuous, the linen spotless, the cutlery and glassware impeccable."

"It seems somewhat verbose and pretentious," I said.

"Two characteristics which are at least conspicuously absent from the modest products of your own pen."

"Thank you. I think. Does he ever get around to mentioning the bill of fare?"

"Read on."

> *The food, on the other hand, can only be described as execrable. My devoted readers will no doubt recall that it is my custom to always order* la specialite d'hote *and the most expensive item on the wine list. The latter, a Chateau Leoville Bordeaux 1864, was excellent, and, indeed, was the only element of the entire experience which prevented me from running screaming into the night.*

"I think the point is made. He doesn't recommend the place. Does anybody pay attention to this pompous windbag?"

"Oh, you'd be surprised," said Holmes. "Apparently, there are quite a few people in polite society who regard his convoluted verbiage as 'good writing' and hang on his every word."

He sighed.

"Well, it provided me with a minute or two of harmless amusement. Anything of interest in *The Telegraph*?"

"Nothing that would concern you, or I would have brought it to your attention."

I glanced across at the clock on the mantelpiece.

"It's only a quarter-to-nine, Holmes. Who knows what the day may bring?"

No sooner were the words out of my mouth than there was a ring at the doorbell, and within minutes we were plunged into a case of paramount importance which, after the passage of a suitable amount of time, may be the subject of one of these narratives. It was, in any event, of sufficient urgency and complexity to drive any remaining thought of Raymond Arnoux completely out of our minds, and it wasn't until several months later that he was thrust once more into our attention, and we found ourselves investigating the murder of the restaurant critic of *The Daily Courier.*

Regular readers of these humble sketches may have noticed that my distinguished friend had a certain affinity with France, and the French. His maternal grandmother had been the sister of the famous French artist, Horace Vernet. His knowledge of French literature far exceeded his acquaintance with that of England, and he could quote freely from Flaubert, Zola, and Georges Sand. And it should be noted that while he refused a knighthood from the English Crown on more than one occasion, he was happy to accept the Order of the *Legion d'Honneur* from the French President, in recognition of his vital part in the arrest of Huret, the infamous boulevard assassin.

One of the ways in which this Gallic connection manifested itself was in a liking for French food. We did not dine out exclusively in French restaurants, but we could usually be found in such establishments two or three times a month. One particular favourite of Holmes was *L'Escargot D'Argent* – in English, *The Silver Snail.* It was small, tucked away in a cul-de-sac in Covent Garden called Little Burbage Street. As well as the attractions of its excellent food, it was a convenient place to dine because of its proximity to the Opera House.

Holmes had had no clients for a week, and I had suggested to him that as a means of occupying himself, he should finish a monograph he had left half-completed on the specialized argots of various professions. He acceded, and spent the next two days researching the subject, riffling through his records of past cases, his own and others', and making copious notes. At last he put pen to paper, and late in the afternoon he stood up from his desk and stretched his long arms.

"You've finished it?" I asked.

"Well, I shall read it through once more tomorrow morning before I send it to the publisher, but I am certainly done for today. How does the idea of an evening out appeal to you?"

"Very much."

Holmes rang the bell, and when Mrs. Hudson appeared, he informed her that we wouldn't be in for dinner, a courtesy which, it has to be said, he didn't always extend to her.

We made our leisurely way on foot to Little Burbage Street, the evening being fresh and clear.

L'Escargot d'Argent was founded, owned, and managed by one Theophile Dumont, who had come to London in 1872. Born in Le Havre, he had fought in the Franco-Prussian War. He survived several of the great battles of that conflict with a few wounds, none of them with any permanent effects other than scars, and after the Battle of Sedan he decided that rather than remain in a country suffering the ill-effects of defeat, he would go to London. He was charmed by the ambience of Covent

Garden and its environs and decided to open a restaurant there, which he did with some financial assistance from his parents. Two old friends from his student days, Maurice Leclerc and Alphonse Duvivier, came from Paris to join him as chef and head waiter. Within two years, all had married Englishwomen, assuring their permanent residence in the capital and the continued existence of L'Escargot d'Argent. The place was not, as yet, well known, but had numerous regular patrons, which maintained its success.

It was relatively small for a restaurant, being of enough size to accommodate some twenty diners at one time. The walls were faced with pine and decorated simply with framed photographs of Parisian locales, theatrical posters, and the occasional painting donated by the artist, for, like his fellow-restaurateurs across the Channel, Dumont would often accept a work of art in lieu of payment for a meal. The furniture was of a basic design, and the tablecloths were cotton checkerboards of red and white.

Alphonse Duvivier was a short, slim individual with black hair smoothed to the back of his head and an impressive waxed moustache that ended in two diminutive curls. When Holmes and I entered the restaurant, he came up and greeted us effusively.

"Ah, Monsieur Holmes! And Doctor Watson! Once more you honour us with your presence! It is very pleasant to see you again! Marcel!" he said, clicking his fingers to summon one of the white-uniformed waiters who were gliding efficiently between the tables with their trays of food and wine.

"You remember the famous detective and his colleague?"

"*Bien sur*. Good evening, gentlemen."

Marcel was also somewhat below average height and, like his superior, sported a moustache. His accent was not that of a Parisian, but I couldn't place it.

"Show Mr. Holmes and Doctor Watson to the window table, and take their order."

After we were comfortably seated, and the little waiter had hurried off to fetch a bottle of wine to accompany our meals, Holmes smiled and said, "Marseilles."

"I beg your pardon?"

"Marcel is from Marseilles, in the *departement* of Bouches-du-Rhone. As I have said many times, your face is an extremely accurate barometer of your thoughts. Marcel has seen us here before, but has never served us, so you hadn't heard him speak. You know that Alphonse is Parisian, and I could see that you were a little puzzled by the difference in accents."

He then gave a brief discourse, to which I listened avidly, on the regions of the French nation and the variations in stress, intonation, and modulation to be found in the accents of each of them.

The waiter returned with our wine and two plates of *vichyssoise*, which we consumed in silence. Then, during the main course, Holmes drew my attention to a new poster on one of the walls, and we embarked on a conversation which began with the career of Jean-Eugène Robert-Houdin and wandered from there to the conquests of the Roman Emperor Aurelian and the likely effects of devaluation on any given currency. I was about to express my own thoughts on the latter subject when the character of the evening was radically changed.

Two men had entered L'Escargot D'Argent while Holmes and I were eating our *vichyssoise*, and I had glanced idly over at them as one of the waiters seated them at a table near the back of the restaurant.

The first was a slim, dapper man of the middle height. The uniform colour and sheen of his thick black hair led one to suspect that they were the result of dye. His features were regular, but his facial expression was one of barely suppressed disdain. His companion appeared to be about ten years older and was about the same height, but rather rotund. His clothes were neither as well-fitting nor of as good quality as that of his companions, and he was carrying a little leather briefcase. His hair was greying, with a distinct bald patch at the back, and I had the impression that for some reason he wasn't comfortable with his surroundings.

After a few minutes, the hum of conversation in the restaurant came to an abrupt end as both men uttered piercing cries. The first slid to the floor and lay prostrate, while the other fell forward onto the table a moment later, his arms outstretched. Heads were turned in curiosity and stayed fixed in horror.

"It seems there is work for us," said Holmes, rising to his feet. "Come, Watson."

Together we hurried to the table where the two men lay inert. I knelt beside the man on the floor and felt his neck for a pulse. There was none. I stood and performed the same action on the other.

"This man is still alive. We must call an ambulance."

"And the police," said Holmes. "Did they have soup?" he asked the white-faced young waiter who had served the pair.

"They both started with *vichyssoise*, and then they had *tournedos Rossini*. And they shared a bottle of Pinot Noir."

Holmes nodded. The bottle of wine stood half-finished on the table, and the two men had clearly just started eating the tournedos.

"The soup plates will have been washed, I suppose."

"Not necessarily, Monsieur Holmes, but there will be a pile of them, and it will be impossible to say which came from this table."

One of the other diners rose and questioned Holmes. "Is it poison?"

"That would seem to be the most likely cause of death," he admitted.

"Food poisoning? Are we all in danger?"

"They had exactly the same meal, but whatever it was is unlikely to have been in the main course, because they had hardly eaten any," said Holmes. He then turned and addressed everyone present "Did anyone else have the *tournedos Rossini*?"

Several diners had, but had eaten them and gone on to their desserts with no ill-effects.

"That leaves the *vichyssoise* and the wine."

"Surely it must have been the wine," I said. "We both had the *vichyssoise*, and we're unharmed, to say nothing of all the others here who must have had it."

"If he has been poisoned," said one of the waiters, gesturing to the unconscious man at the table, "shouldn't we give him something to make him bring it up?"

"No, no," I interjected quickly, "that would be the worst thing to do. We don't know yet what type of poison it was, if it was. When it comes back up it could get into his lungs, or damage his oesophagus. They'll know what to do at the hospital."

A horse-drawn vehicle from the St. John Ambulance Brigade arrived to take the survivor to University College Hospital, followed shortly by the police in the person of one Inspector Lanner, an alert, eager young Scotland Yard Inspector who had called on Holmes for assistance more than once in the recent past. He was accompanied by his sergeant, Ross, a burly ex-military man, and two uniformed constables.

The next to arrive was Theophile Dumont, a tall, imposing man with the traditional ample girth of the successful restaurateur. He hadn't been present at the restaurant but entered now, in an advanced state of agitation, having been summoned by Alphonse. He went from table to table, assuring the customers that under the circumstances they wouldn't be charged for their meal. On reaching the table where we sat, he seized Holmes's hand and cried, "Ah, praise be to *le bon Dieu* that you are here! I confess, I don't trust your English police. But you, Monsieur Holmes, surely you can solve this crime and save my restaurant from shame and ruin?"

Holmes gently disengaged his hand from Dumont's.

"I'm afraid that we must leave the matter to the official force for the time being. If they cannot find the culprit, I promise that I will take up the case. At the moment, however, Monsieur Dumont, I am afraid that Dr. Watson and I are merely witnesses."

Holmes stayed in communication with Lanner for the next week. That was how we learned that the murdered man was restaurant critic Raymond Arnoux. The other man, Charles Morgan, had the same occupation, writing for another newspaper, *The Daily Clarion*. The remaining wine, and the two glasses, had been examined and yielded no trace of poison, although the police autopsy had confirmed that this was the cause of death. The lethal substance was *botulin*, which has the twin advantages, so far as the malefactor is concerned, of being both odourless and tasteless, and easily manufactured, so that unlike arsenic, for example, it need not be purchased at a chemist's, where a record would be made of its sale.

At the end of the week, Lanner called on us, looking rather haggard and woebegone.

"I have my theories, Mr. Holmes," he said, as he took a seat in our living-room, "but no solid evidence to back them up."

Holmes reached for one of his pipes and filled the bowl with tobacco.

"Pray tell me what they are, then," he said, striking a match.

"Well," the inspector began, "French-speaking waiters are a close-knit group. There cannot be more than a hundred of them in the whole of London. Arnoux is at least indirectly responsible for the failure of quite a few restaurants over the last few years. A brother, or a close friend, or the murderer himself, loses a job when one fails, and the killer fixates on the person he holds responsible. The waiter comes to work at L'Escargot d'Argent, and when Arnoux books a table, the murderer sees his time has come."

"Is that feasible?" I asked.

"Oh, yes," said Holmes. "And in terms of motive, waiters who have been employed by the same restaurant for a long time can feel a great sense of loyalty toward the place, and their employers. Ask Alphonse Duvivier. Presumably you have questioned the waiter who served Morgan and Arnoux?"

"Thoroughly, and he would seem to be in the clear. He has only worked there for two weeks, and in fact has only been in London for three. I sent his name and description to the *Sûreté*, and they confirmed his identity. The other person I concentrated on was the chef, Maurice Leclerc, and he most definitely had a motive, of the kind I mentioned earlier. His younger brother had had followed him to London and was employed as the chef at the Auberge de Jehan Cottard, which closed down not long after Arnoux gave it a particularly scathing review, and after that no other restaurateur would employ him."

It was at that point that I recalled the conversation Holmes and had had some months before, and it struck me that to one of a passionate Gallic temperament, that might indeed be motive enough for murder.

"I questioned him long and hard," continued Lanner, "but he didn't break."

"The problem is method, not motive, at least for the moment," said Holmes. "How did the botulin get into the soup, for that is surely where the poison was? If it was done by the chef, or by the waiter, it is difficult to see how it could be carried out without the complicity of the other. The waiter knows to whom he is serving the soup, but how does he get the lethal dose into it without being sure that he will not be seen? True, he is in the middle of the busy kitchen, or the equally busy restaurant, but he is either holding one plate in each hand, or bearing both on a tray. The poison is presumably in a vial or some other small receptacle which he must take from a pocket and pour into the *vichyssoise*. How can he do that without setting down the plates?

"Now let us consider the chef. You will recall that *vichyssoise* is served with a garnish of chopped chives, which is added just before serving the soup. Under cover of this action, it would be easy for him to add the poison. The problem then would be that, unless the waiter were an accomplice, the chef couldn't possibly be sure that the poisoned soup would go to the correct table."

"But why poison both of them," I objected, "if Arnoux was his target?"

"Possibly the killer didn't know him by sight," said Lanner. "He'd have to kill both of them to be sure of Arnoux's death."

"A reasonable assumption," said Holmes.

"Kill an innocent man to ensure the death of a guilty one?" I expostulated.

"It would hardly be without precedent," replied Holmes, "and recent history provides us with several examples. In

Adelaide in 1879, Thomas Hawkins killed a pair of twin brothers. He discovered that one of them had seduced his sister, to whom he had an unhealthy attachment. She sought to protect her lover by pretending she didn't know which twin it was, so he murdered both of them. Then there's the case of Sven Jorgenson in Stockholm in '83. He poisoned a dinner party of twelve people by putting strychnine in the dessert. It was revealed at the trial that he only had a motive for killing one of them. And only last year, the case of Wing Fat in San Francisco was along similar lines. But let us not forget, Charles Morgan is still alive, is he not, Lanner?"

"He's still in University College Hospital. They'll be letting him out in a few days, apparently."

The next morning Holmes stood up immediately after breakfast and put on his light summer jacket.

"You are going out?" I inquired.

"Yes, to Scotland Yard, and then to L'Escargot D'Argent."

"You have, then, some clue to the solution of this mystery?"

"Like our friend Lanner, I have a theory which must be put to the test. If it rings true, then I will ask you to accompany me to University College Hospital this afternoon. That is, of course, unless you have more pressing business of your own to conduct."

"Holmes, you know full well that I am currently without a practice," I said with not a little irritation.

"So, I can rely on your presence. Until this afternoon, then."

Having lived with Holmes for this long, I was, I presume,

more sensitive to his changing moods than any other man alive, but I confess that when he returned to Baker Street at about two o'clock, I found it difficult to discern his frame of mind. As we rattled in a hansom through the crowded streets of London en route to the hospital, it seemed to me that behind his stoic mask there were signs of both triumph and frustration. No doubt, I told myself, there would be answers at our destination. And so it proved.

There was a middle-aged nurse on duty at the hospital reception desk. Holmes gave her his most winning smile and said, "May we see Charles Morgan? We are friends of his, and we have his briefcase."

I had of course noticed what he had been carrying, but as I had seen it only briefly at the restaurant, I hadn't made the connection. Now he held it up so that the nurse could see the little letters "*C.M..*" where they were embossed into the leather surface just below the closed flap.

"He left it at the restaurant that night. Understandably. How is he?"

"He's still a bit weak, but well enough to have visitors. He's in a private room on the second floor. 24-A."

We climbed the stairs and found the room. Morgan lay on his back in bed, dressed in a blue-and-white hospital gown and in a state of half-sleep. He looker older and fatter, and more out of shape than he had in his suit in the restaurant

"Morgan!" Holmes said in a loud, clear voice. The journalist sat up and rubbed his bleary eyes.

"What is it?" he said. "Who are you?"

"You may have heard of us. I am Sherlock Holmes, and this is my friend and colleague Dr. John Watson. You left your briefcase behind at L'Escargot D'Argent. I had to go to Scotland Yard to pick it up. They thought it might be evidence."

"Oh, thank you. But evidence of what?"

"There were a couple of things in it. The police couldn't understand, but to me those two things suggest, although it cannot be proven, that you killed Raymond Arnoux."

Morgan's face twisted into a mask of contempt.

"What on earth are you talking about? Killed him? I nearly died myself."

"Yes, and it seemed odd to me that a man both older and demonstrably less healthy should survive when a younger, fitter man succumbed. You put your own life at risk in order to take his. That indicates a powerful hatred. What was it, Morgan? Professional jealousy of a richer, more successful restaurant critic? A woman, perhaps, whom you wanted and he had? You may as well tell me. I have already told you I can't prove anything."

"I'm telling you nothing." Morgan paused. "There's nothing to tell. And even if there were, I'm not stupid enough to say it in front of two people. That would be tantamount to a confession."

"Very well." Holmes opened the briefcase and reached into it. "Exhibits *A* and *B*."

Morgan gave a false laugh.

"A pair of soup spoons? Are you insane? What does that

64

prove?"

"Let us use the word 'suggest' rather than 'prove'. As you say, two soup spoons, from L'Escargot D'Argent. And, like all the cutlery in that establishment – " Holmes turned them so that Morgan could see the backs of the handles. " – stamped with the letters '*E*' and '*A*'. Now, I went back to the restaurant this morning and, with the kind permission of the manager, examined all the spoons. I found two that had plain backs." Morgan arched one eyebrow sardonically.

"And what does that 'suggest' to you?"

"It suggests that when you arrived at the restaurant, you had the two plain-handled spoons in your briefcase. You had coated them both with botulin. You had them in separate compartments so that you knew which had the fatal, and which the non-fatal dose. At some point you replaced the restaurant spoons with the poisoned ones, not realising that they weren't identical. Perhaps Arnoux unwittingly made it easier for you by going to the men's room. He ordered first, and you had the same. You knew that by the time the botulin took effect, the spoons would either have been washed or be lying in a pile with many others waiting to be washed, and indistinguishable from them at a casual glance."

"Bravo," said Morgan. "An excellent piece of fiction."

"You are neither as clever nor as original as you may imagine. You are hardly the first murderer by poison who has taken a dose himself to throw the law off the scent. There was Coleraine in Bristol in 1854, and Steiner in Metz in 1873, to cite just two examples. You have escaped punishment on this occasion, but – " Holmes moved a little closer to the bed and lifted an admonitory finger. " – be warned. My eyes are upon you. If you perpetrate any other such crime, I will not hesitate to take the law into my own hands and punish you accordingly."

"Both those eventualities seem unlikely," said Morgan with an unpleasant smile. "And now, I'd like to sleep. Please leave."

I accompanied Holmes out into the cold, antiseptic corridor. I was chilled by the implication of his last words to Morgan, but said nothing. I knew he had spoken the strict truth, for justice was his concern, not the letter of the law.

Holmes informed Lanner of his conclusions, and the inspector agreed that under the circumstances, nothing could be done. Nevertheless, the tale has a sequel. After Arnoux's death, Morgan became the restaurant critic of *The Daily Courier*. Had he known that he would be the likely successor to the dead man's position? Had he feigned friendship and invited Arnoux to L'Escargot D'Argent with that result in mind? Two weeks after starting with his new paper, a fire broke out at a restaurant he had been sent to review. The crowded dining room of Il Piatto d'Oro had suddenly filled with billowing smoke, and although some of the diners had gone to hospital suffering from smoke inhalation, none of them had died. None, that is, except for Charles Morgan.

As for Theophile Dumont, the unsolved murder didn't destroy his restaurant business, as he had expected. In fact, so many people were interested to dine at the establishment where it had taken place that he was obliged to expand L'Escargot

D'Argent and bring in more tables. Even after twenty years, Dumont exclaimed, he still didn't understand the English character.

The Adventure of the
Surrey Revenant

The year of 1894, which had seen the return of Mr. Sherlock Holmes to 221b Baker Street, and his resumption of his role of consulting detective and last court of appeal, was drawing to a close. The seven months since he had brought Professor Moriarty's deputy, the formidable Colonel Sebastian Moran, to justice, had been amongst the busiest of his professional career, and I had been privileged to accompany and assist him on many of his most important cases, even as I had in those days before his seeming death amid the swirling waters of the Reichenbach Falls.

I had left our lodgings on a brief shopping expedition in search of a new razor, my old one, which I had bought shortly before my attachment to the Fifth Northumberland Fusiliers, having given up the ghost after many years' service. As I climbed the steps to our rooms on my return I heard Holmes's clear, high voice coming through the door. I had passed Mrs. Hudson in the hallway, so he was presumably conversing with a client.

"I'm very sorry, Mr. Bridges, but I don't think I can take your case. While you have my complete sympathy, I think you should consult an exorcist, or at any rate a priest of some kind. Your situation really doesn't come within my purview. Ah, good morning, Watson."

I had entered our sitting room and saw what appeared to be a sane and competent middle-aged member of the rentier class, respectably dressed and well groomed, his straight brown hair neatly combed to the back of his head and his upper lip adorned with a meticulously trimmed moustache.

"Am I interrupting?" I asked.

"No, Doctor, I believe Mr. Bridges is about to leave."

Bridges rose to his feet, his regular features writhing in frustration.

"I came to you because I was told you help people – those who cannot go to the police. People who need things kept out of the papers. People who have nowhere else to go. Obviously I was misinformed. Good day, sir."

"I, at least, would like to hear your story, Mr. Bridges," I interrupted. "Surely there is no harm in that, Holmes."

The detective leaned forward in his chair.

"Please sit down, Mr. Bridges. Perhaps I was a little hasty. I have rather more human weaknesses than one might imagine from reading about me in my friend's accounts of our cases. But you would admit that most people, hearing your story, would find it incredible, and might well come to the conclusion that you were, at the very least, suffering from some kind of delusion. Surely the simplest and most logical solution to the situation is that it was a case of mistaken identity."

"I've known the man for twenty years, I tell you. It was him, not just somebody who looked like him. And as I said, I've seen him more than once."

69

"Excuse me, gentlemen," I interjected, "but I have yet to hear the story."

"My apologies, Watson. Please repeat what you have told me, Mr. Bridges, and I assure you I shall make no more observations until you have finished."

He reached for his pipe and Persian slipper, and Michael Bridges began his tale.

"Fifteen years ago, I started a business with my friend, Arthur Atwell. We specialised in the production of agricultural machinery. I don't suppose you've heard of us, but amongst farming folk, Atwell and Bridges have a pretty solid reputation. Do you know anything about Haiti, Dr. Watson?"

"Beyond the fact that it is part of the island of Hispaniola, I know virtually nothing of it. Why do you ask?"

"Well, most people don't even know that much. After a rough time of political and social chaos, Michel Domingue introduced a fairer and more democratic constitution in 1874, resulting in a stability which has lasted to this day. In such circumstances, one can usually expect to see an improvement in agriculture, with greater efficiency and higher yields. But Haiti has virtually no industry, and is consequently unable to produce the machinery which would facilitate this. Now, Arthur and I always kept an eye out for potential new markets, and we came up with a plan for Haiti which we believed would be beneficial to both parties. We would sell them our products at greatly reduced prices in exchange for a guaranteed percentage of the profits from their exported goods."

"That sounds like an eminently sensible scheme," I remarked.

"Well, we thought so too. Most of the small-holding farmers there are dirt poor, but we were sure that there were enough big landowners who were rich enough to be interested in what we had to offer, and would have some influence in government circles. The only way to meet those landowners and convince them was for one of us to go to Haiti in person. Arthur was always better at that sort of thing, so he went. It was a long journey – Portsmouth to New York by sea, New York to Miami by train, and then Miami to Port-au-Prince by boat. I received a letter from him, posted a few days after he arrived, telling me that not only had we made a big mistake, but he was in personal danger and was returning home as soon as he could and catching the first available boat to Miami. The mistake we had made was that the landowners had hundreds of people working the land for them, using primitive methods and in conditions of virtual slavery, and the owners liked it that way. So Arthur had to get out, and he did get out, but not alive. It was his dead body that took that long journey back."

"Was there a death certificate?"

"Yes, Arthur's son and daughter made the journey to Port-au-Prince as soon as the news reached them from the British representative there, and it was given directly into their hands. The cause of death was diagnosed as a heart attack. I couldn't believe that at first. Arthur was fifty-five, a few years older than me, but he was pretty fit for a man of his age. But then I thought,

71

he had that long journey, all that time in a hot country, the failure of our enterprise, the threat of death, and even eating food he wasn't used to – all that must have combined to put a strain on his heart. I must confess, I felt – and feel – rather guilty. I should have gone. I'm not married, you see, and I've no one to grieve over me.

"That's the background, but it's time I came to the point. The part you won't believe – that Mr. Holmes here already doesn't believe. It was dark, and I had just been to see Edgar and Amelia, Arthur's children, in Sutton in Surrey, about ten days ago. I suppose it was about eleven at night. I'd gone over there with some documents connected with the business that they needed to sign. The door of their house is at the end of a narrow cul-de-sac, so I had parked the carriage on the main road near the other end of it and now I was walking back down the street. I heard footsteps behind me. I turned, and someone came out of the darkness into the light of a streetlamp, and I thought my own heart was going to stop when I saw Arthur's face. His face, I swear it, but deathly pale and bearing an expression of unutterable horror. His eyes seemed to be staring into the very pits of Hell. I scuttled backwards away from him, then I turned back and ran off as far and as fast as I could."

He took a couple of deep breaths then continued. "I found a cab and got home. The next day, I told my coachman to go and fetch the carriage. I couldn't stand to go back there."

"Why didn't he drive you the night before?" I asked.

"It was his night off, that's all. Wednesday night. I didn't tell anyone what had happened. As you said, if I told most people, they'd think I was insane."

Holmes broke his silence.

"I didn't say that, exactly."

"Well, my own first thought was that I was going mad. I tried to tell myself I'd been tired, or overwrought because of Arthur's death, or that I'd drunk too much while dining with Edgar and Amelia, but none of that was true. If I wasn't insane, the only alternative was that it was really him. I'd had a supernatural experience. Do you know what a zombie is?"

"I've heard the word, that's all," I said, "but perhaps you can enlighten me."

"Certainly. I have done some research into the matter in the past few days. If Arthur had died in Haiti, then the root of the situation was to be found there. As you may know, the religion of Haiti is voodooism. There is no central authority, no Pope or Archbishop, which I imagine stems from the fact that the Negroes who were transported there as slaves came from many different tribal cultures. Their priests are called *houngans*, and some of them are good and virtuous, while others, known as *bokors*, follow what some call 'The Left Hand Path'."

"That of evil."

"Precisely. The *houngans* disinter dead bodies and reanimate them by the use of magical rituals. In this state of half-life, they can perform simple duties for long hours, needing no food or sleep. Being turned into a zombie is a form of punishment.

Instead of being borne to the realm of the *loa*, the gods, the perpetrator of a crime – rape, say, or murder – is resurrected from the grave to a living death and condemned to carry out the most menial or irksome tasks until the *houngan* who has created the zombie, or his successor, deems that the zombie has expiated his or her crime."

His use of language suggested that he was quoting verbatim from a book, or books, on the subject.

"My opinion is that the large landowners on Haiti form a small group of *bokors*, or have some working on their behalf, who turn the innocent dead into zombies to use as workers in their fields. You can't get cheaper labour than that – they don't need food, they don't get sick or ask for improved pay and conditions. That would also explain why the landowners rejected our offer."

"You mentioned earlier that you had seen your friend more than once since his death," said Holmes,

"Yes. The second occasion was in the garden of my house in St. John's Wood, the night before last. I was awakened by the garden gate banging at about one in the morning and went down to close it. Arthur stepped out of the shadow of the trees into the moonlight. I wasn't quite as scared this time, because, as I said, now I had an explanation of sorts."

"Did you try to speak to him?"

"I called him by name, and his expression lightened a little, but zombies only fully respond to the one who has been given power over them."

"And you alone heard the garden gate making a noise?"

"My bedroom is on that side of the house. The servants" rooms are all on the other side."

"Did you try to restrain him?"

"Certainly not! Zombies are possessed of preternatural strength. He would have torn me to pieces. No, I let him go, by the garden gate."

"You didn't attempt to follow him?"

"Follow a zombie and their master becomes aware of you? You don't want that to happen."

"Even though they are on the other side of the Atlantic Ocean?" I asked. I confess that I was beginning to find Mr. Bridges' apparent gullibility somewhat irksome.

"It seemed quite possible to me that it might be the work of someone in this country, who had made a deeper study of voodoo. Or, of course, a native *bokor* could have come here by ship."

"Just a few more questions, Mr. Bridges," continued Holmes. "First, do you know where Mr. Atwell is – or rather *was* – buried?"

"In the churchyard of St. Botolph's, near the house in Surrey."

"Which now belongs to his son and daughter?"

"Yes."

"When?"

"The first available day after his body arrived. I was at the funeral. A Saturday, it must have been."

"The Saturday before the Wednesday you first saw him?"

"Yes."

"Did you see Atwell's body before it was interred?"

"No, the coffin was closed. Apparently the facial distortion caused by the pain of the sudden heart attack was beyond the ability of the undertakers to alter, because *rigor mortis* had set in during the transportation of the corpse."

"And his grave is now empty, if your suspicions are correct."

"An exhumation order would prove that one way or another," I said, "but I doubt the authorities would credit the reasons for requesting one. Why do you suppose he has appeared to you, and not his children?"

"We were great friends, don't forget."

"But what do you think he, or whoever may be controlling him, wants of you?" asked Holmes.

"I couldn't say."

"Did you and Mr. Atwood have any enemies?"

"Business rivals, certainly, but none of them knew about Arthur's trip to Haiti. Even if they had, I can't imagine any of them being behind this."

"No others?"

"None that I am aware of."

"Have you visited Mr. Atwood's children since that Wednesday?

"Yes. They invited me again the following Wednesday. All the papers transferring their father's interest in the business to them have been signed and dealt with, but since Arthur's death I think I may have become something of a substitute father for them."

"Did you drive the carriage again?"

"No, this time I asked my coachman to drive me there. He was a little put out, as Wednesday is also his lady friend's night off, but he agreed when I promised him the whole weekend free. He drove me to dinner, and I left at eleven again."

"Now, lastly," said Holmes, "what do you require of us? That we wait with you for a further visitation and witness that your tale is true? Or that we track down whoever is behind this?"

"Oh, no, Mr. Holmes. I want you to help me kill him – or rather, destroy him, since he's already dead. Put him out of his misery. As an old friend, it's the least I can do."

"I see. We shall give you whatever assistance you need, but first I shall give you some instructions you must follow to the letter. Do you have any other residence besides your house in St. John's Wood?"

"Yes, I have a cottage just outside Studley in Warwickshire."

"Excellent. I take it you can leave your business to run itself for a few days?"

"I have a very reliable man who is often left in charge."

"Then here is what you must do: Go home and pack a suitcase, then go to your office and inform them that you will be at your cottage from the eighth onwards – "

"But today is the fourth."

" – and then return here and give me the keys to the property in St. John's Wood, not forgetting to provide us with the address. Then take the first available train to Studley. Tell no one else of your departure. Stay there until we arrive on the seventh."

"But what is your plan, sir?"

"Mr. Bridges, if I am to bring this matter to a satisfactory conclusion, then you must trust me and allow me to keep my own counsel. Mrs. Hudson will show you out."

Reaching across to the bell-pull, he rang to summon that estimable lady.

"Thank you, Watson, If not for your timely arrival, I might have missed out on what looks to be a most interesting case. Mr. Bridges clearly found you a more sympathetic listener, as he told his story at greater length and in more detail than when I was his sole audience. By the way, I trust your quest for a new razor was successful."

"Yes, I went to Hayworth's in the Bayswater Road. But how – ?"

My hand flew up to my face.

"Relax, my friend. Your shave is but an hour or two overdue, and only the trained eye of one who knows of your habits would notice the very slight stubble on your cheeks and chin. Your reputation for scrupulous neatness remains intact. Now, what do you make of Bridges' story?"

"I find it very surprising that an apparently sane man could credit such nonsense for a single moment."

"Well, Watson, a rich vein of supernaturalism runs beneath the surface of our scientific, mechanized society, and as belief in the established religion wanes, folk become susceptible to more *outré* modes of thought. You and I are agreed that these visitations cannot be due to necromancy. How then, may we explain them?"

I thought for a few seconds.

"There is a certain amount of evidence that persons of a hypersensitive nature may be prone to hallucinations, particularly where the individual is suffering from a strong negative emotion, such as guilt."

"There were certainly a few indications that there is more to Mr. Bridges than his stolid exterior would suggest. Anything else?"

"Both these events took place at night. Perhaps whoever is behind this found someone who resembled Atwell enough to pass for him in a bad light. Or even," I continued, warming to the theme, "someone took a cast of his face after death and used it to construct a mask of rubber that would serve a similar purpose. Bridges did say that Atwell's face had an unnatural pallor."

Holmes looked down with a fixed, introspective look in his grey eyes.

"No," he said after a few seconds, "no. There is something else at work here, something deeper."

He looked up at me once more.

"Are you aware, Watson, that some have explained the Greek legend of the Centaurs by saying that they were simply men on horseback, as seen through the eyes of those who had never encountered such riders before?"

"I'm sorry, Holmes, I don't see your point."

"If zombies exist – "

"Oh, come now, Holmes!"

" – then there must be a rational, scientific explanation for their existence."

"If there is one, I have no doubt that you of all men can find it out. But what is our first move? I take it you were not serious when you agreed to help him destroy whoever or whatever it was he saw."

"I would if there were an absolute necessity for such action, but I think it highly unlikely that there will be. You realize, of course, that I sent him off to his cottage in Warwickshire principally to get him out of the way?"

"I imagined that was the reason."

"The presence of one who is convinced of the supernatural nature of these visits, to say nothing of his murderous intent, would hamper our investigation. Here is what we shall do: After Bridges has returned with the key and departed for the station, we will go to his house and take up temporary residence there until the seventh. If we see no zombies, we shall take the train to Studley and stay with our client until we see one there, though I have greater hopes of St. John's Wood."

"And during the days?"

"I will spend the first at the Reading Room at the British Museum, consulting Eckermann and whatever else I can find of relevance. And have no fear. When the hour of action does arrive, your presence will be crucial, or I should not have asked you to come."

Michael Bridges returned a couple of hours later with the key to 83 Perceval Gardens, St. John's Wood.

"I will give you a note to take to my servants," said Bridges when Holmes informed him of our plans regarding his house.

"Servants, indeed," I remarked as I gazed out of one of the windows at our client climbing into his carriage on the street below us.

"You heard him say so earlier. It is hardly remarkable that a rich man would have them."

"True. Has he any inkling of the reason we are sending him out of London, do you think?"

"As long as he obeys my instructions, it is immaterial to me whether he has or not. Now, Watson, have you packed enough for our short stay?"

"Of course."

"And I have already informed Mrs. Hudson of our impending absence, so we can be off without delay, and you can christen your new razor in the bathroom of 83 Perceval Gardens."

Bridge's house was a fully-detached villa-style building of the late eighteenth century with a large L-shaped garden that ran along its left side and back. Between the wall separating the garden from the next-door neighbour and the front of the house ran a set of iron railings with a wrought-iron gate at the centre. Rather than using the key Bridges had given him, Holmes rapped on the door with its brass knocker.

The door was opened by a tall, dark-haired young woman in a maid's outfit.

"Good afternoon," said Holmes.

"Good afternoon, sirs. I am afraid Mr. Bridges is not in."

"He gave us this," said Holmes, proffering the note.

It read:

> *This is to inform you that Mr. Sherlock Holmes and his colleague, Dr. Watson, will be staying at the house for the next few days in my absence. You will obey their orders as you would mine and serve them in the same manner.*
>
> *M.A. Bridges*
> *4th November, 1894*

"Sherlock Holmes!" said the young woman in a tone of awe.

"You have heard of me, then. Perhaps you would bring the rest of the staff here so that we can meet them all."

The household consisted of a butler, a cook, two more maids, and a boot-boy.

The butler, Wheatcroft, had a slight whiff of brown ale about him and his collar was slightly askew, as if it had been buttoned in haste. While the cats away, the mice will play, as the old adage has it. The cook, a dumpy, maternal woman with a Scots accent, was called Mrs. Guthrie. The maid who had opened the door to us was Mortimer, while the other two, both shorter and pale-skinned, answered to Mullins and Ratcliff. Jackson, the boot-boy, was a scrawny, somewhat-underdeveloped youth of sixteen, who looked two or three years younger. There was also the carriage driver, but Bridges has given him the week off.

"Before you go back to your duties," said Holmes, "I have a request to make of you: From tomorrow onward, if anyone calls at the house during the day, whether you know them or not, you are to tell them that your master is from home, but will be back in the evening. Is that clear? Good. You can go now."

"Dinner will be at half-past-seven, sir,"

"Thank you, Mrs. Guthrie."

I came down to dinner after a short rest, freshly shaven, to find Holmes waiting for me. As we ate the excellent three-course meal served us by Mullins and Ratcliff, Holmes informed me of the part I was to play. I had been given the role of Bridges because my moustache made it possible for me to be briefly mistaken for him, and also because my medical experience made me slightly more qualified for the task I must perform.

When we had finished, we repaired to the smoking room and chatted leisurely about other matters unconnected to the business in hand, smoking panatelas and drinking from a decanter of brandy brought to us by Wheatcroft.

Both of the guest bedrooms were on the same side of the house as Bridges' room, so if our visitor announced his presence by banging the gate, at least one of us would be sure to hear it. He did not call on that first night, nor on the second. Both of us were prepared for our separate tasks, but he didn't arrive until one in the morning on the seventh.

When Holmes returned from his researches at about three o'clock on the afternoon of our first full day, I scarcely gave him time to remove his topcoat before I began quizzing him on the subject. I had had a pleasant enough day leafing through the books in Bridges' library, to say nothing of consuming a splendid lunch, but I was most eager to know what he had learned.

Holmes gave me an indulgent smile.

"Background and colour for your coming account of the case, eh?"

"Well, I've given it a little thought, yes."

"Let us at least discuss it in comfort."

I followed him into the spacious living room, where we each sat down in one of the large, mahogany-brown padded-leather armchairs.

"Well, to begin with, voodoo is not just the religion of the common people, but permeates the professional classes there to such a degree that virtually every lawyer, doctor, and landowner is a *houngan*. One might even say that, despite those democratic reforms Bridges mentioned, they are the country's true rulers.

"As to zombies, they are never seen outside their work area, or at night. Unfortunately, discussion of the whole subject is prone to sensationalism, and it is entirely possible that Bridges consulted some unreliable texts. Even those writers I read who seem to believe that zombies are indeed resurrected corpses said nothing about their masters being able to divine where they are when out of sight, nor do they simply appear and disappear like ghosts."

For my part, the event which took place in the morning of the seventh of November, though brief, is indelibly imprinted on my memory. I had stood beside Holmes on more than one occasion when we appeared to be in the presence of the supernatural, and although he had always proved that there was a rational explanation for the phenomenon, nevertheless, each time I had experienced a chilling moment of atavistic fear, during which, for all my scientific and medical training, it seemed to me that such things might somehow, after all, exist.

We heard the banging of the garden gate – in fact, it was opened and closed with a clatter more than once, doubtless to ensure that Bridges would be awakened by the noise. In accordance with our plan, Holmes and I sprang into action. We both hurried down the stairs, and I went into the garden by the back door while Holmes went into the street by the main door. The air was filled with the chill of the late autumn as I took up my position.

A figure moved toward me, its pale, hollowed face ghastly in the circle of light cast by a nearby street lamp, its eyes full of a desperate and terrible sadness. I took a hypodermic syringe from my pocket, but as I raised it to plunge the needle in, the figure caught my arm and held it with an unanticipated burst of strength, such strength as a madman might possess. I flung the whole weight of my body against him, bringing us both to the damp earth. For a moment my hand was free, and I stuck the needle in his neck and depressed the plunger, flooding his system with 300-milligrams of chloral hydrate. For a second or two I feared it had had no effect, but then Atwell fell back in a stupour, his eyes closed and his face somewhat relaxed.

As I pulled myself to my feet, I heard cries and the sounds of a struggle coming from the street.

A minute or so later Holmes appeared, his revolver was in his hand. It was trained upon a tubby, bespectacled young man with his hands cuffed in front of him. He had a hard, spoiled face, and his eyes were filled with malice and frustration, and perhaps fear at what must now lie ahead of him.

"Watson, allow me to introduce Mr. Edgar Atwell, the perpetrator of this little plan."

He reached into the pockets of the man's coat and produced a vial of a colourless liquid.

"Ah, my surmise was correct. You carry an extra supply, in case the last dose proved insufficient. Watson, let us get this fellow inside and restrain him more fully. Then we can bear his unfortunate father inside and lay him on one of the beds."

His arm in Holmes's iron grip, the young man didn't struggle. Once inside, we tied him to a kitchen chair with a length of washing line, and he spoke for the first time, in an unpleasant rasping tone.

"I hope you realize that this is illegal restraint."

"Preventing a criminal's escape isn't illegal. Whereas your treatment of your father is a form of assault, and I don't doubt

86

that a charge of attempted embezzlement can also be laid at your door, at the very least."

We brought the older Atwell inside and laid him on the bed of the room I had been occupying. We then woke Wheatcroft, telling him to summon an ambulance and the police.

While we waited, I said, "What was that liquid you took from young Atwell's pocket?"

"Oh, that? Nothing less than the key to this whole business, and a lot more besides. I'm not yet sure of its chemical composition, but you have seen for yourself what its effects are. Once Atwell Senior has been taken to hospital and his son to the police cells, we must return to Baker Street and analyse it." He took a small bottle from his own pocket and poured half the contents of the vial into it. Seeing my questioning glance, he said, "We must give the police a chance to come to their own conclusions."

We returned to Baker Street the following morning, and while our stay in St. John's Wood had undeniably had its pleasant aspects, I was happy to be back in our humble lodgings, and I was sure that Holmes, who was never completely content when away from his files and reference books, felt the same.

"You played your role to perfection, Watson, said Holmes as we took our accustomed armchairs in our sitting room," and it is only fair that I give you a complete explanation of the case as I understand it."

"May I take notes?"

"Of course."

I went to my desk and pulled a notebook and pencil from a drawer. When I was seated once more, Holmes began.

"Now, as you know, when one is in search of a motive for a crime, a good starting point is the question, "*Cui bono?*", and it seemed to me that the only possible beneficiaries of this situation were Edgar and Amelia Atwell. By getting rid of both their father and Michael Bridges, full ownership of the firm would come into their hands. Their plan had the advantage that all the possible outcomes would serve their ends. If Bridges shared his belief, he might be considered insane – indeed, with sufficient persecution, he might actually *become* insane. In those circumstances, all that remained was to dispose of the father, who was already thought dead. If Bridges killed his partner in the belief that he was saving his soul, again, it wouldn't matter that the victim was already supposed to be dead, there would be a *corpus delicti*, and Edgar on hand as a witness. In fact, they might even claim that the entire hoax had been engineered by Bridges, rather than by them."

"Diabolical!"

"Indeed. My suspicions were supported by several facts. The first visitation took place near the house in Surrey, and Bridges was alone in the quiet street when he saw Atwell. In all probability, he had told the pair in passing that he had driven himself that night, but the following Wednesday, he was with his coachman, and he didn't see the older Atwell. Either he had told the son and daughter of the coachman's presence, or they had made a point of asking him about it. In St. John's Wood, much closer to the centre of the metropolis, Edgar waited until one in the morning for the street to be clear before bringing his father into the garden.

"Then there was the burial. As Atwell Senior hadn't died, of a heart attack or anything else, I think it likely that he was secreted somewhere in the house, and the coffin was full of stones, or perhaps even a genuine corpse they had somehow obtained. Let us not forget that even before this plan went into action, they received a considerable allowance from their father, enough to indulge in some selective bribery."

"And still that wasn't enough for them. They wanted it all."

"Quite. Now, as I told you before, the professional classes in Haiti are almost exclusively comprised of *houngans*. The Atwells might have obtained a falsified death certificate, and a supply of that liquid you saw me take from Edgar's pocket, from a corrupt medical man. I believe that they crossed the Atlantic before they claimed to have, once they learned their father was *en route*. That is, something that can be confirmed or disproved by the shipping lines" records of passengers to New York. Whether they formulated their plan in London, or during the crossing, or created it with the aid of a *houngan*, or perhaps more correctly a *bokor*, remains to be seen."

"You have yet to tell me exactly what that liquid was."

"Have you heard of the puffer fish?"

"It is poisonous, is it not?"

"Well, parts of it are edible. Those are known to the Japanese as *fugu*, and can only be prepared by specially trained chefs who know exactly which parts of the fish to cook. The rest contain a deadly neurotoxin called *tetrodotoxin*. If you eat the liver, for example, or the skin, you will die very quickly, and in great pain. Well, the *genus* the pufferfish belong to, the *tetraodontidae*, are found all over the world, including the Caribbean, and many of them have the same toxic properties as the pufferfish. What about *datura*? Do you know what that is?"

"No, I am afraid you have me there."

"It's also known as Devil's Trumpet – Jimson Weed, Hell's Bells, Thorn Apple, and a few other colourful names. Whatever name you give it, it's a plant which also contains deadly toxins. In smaller doses, it can cause hallucinations and temporary paralysis. The liquid in that vial contained both tetrodotoxin and tropane alkaloids, the active ingredient of *datura*, in significant amounts. It is my belief, though I will need to consult a neurologist to be completely sure, that in the right combination they would produce the classic zombie state, which Atwell manifested. Suspension of the higher brain functions with the autonomic system unaffected. To maintain this state, one would need to dose the subject on a regular basis, and if this dosage is stopped, he or she should eventually revert to normal."

"So Arthur Atwell will recover?"

"That is to be hoped for, but I don't envy him on the day he finds out what his own children did to him and Bridges. '*How sharper than a serpent's tooth it is, to have a thankless child!*' as Shakespeare says in *King Lear*. Now, before I forget, we must send a telegram to Studley and summon Mr. Bridges back to London.

Contrary to Holmes's hopes, Arthur Atwell never fully recovered. His mental faculties permanently impaired, he was placed in a private nursing home. Michael Bridges was ready to pay for his care, but the costs were instead met by an anonymous donor, with the condition that Bridges never visit his old friend.

Neither of the Atwell siblings was ever brought to trial. When the police arrived at the house in Surrey to question Amelia, she was nowhere to be found. Her brother's failure to return must have warned her that the game was up, and she fled to save her own skin. As to Edgar, we heard no more of him once we had handed him over into police custody.

These codas to our investigations would have struck both Holmes and I as odd, had it not been for an event which took place a few days after the case was concluded, and from which much might be inferred.

We had just finished our lunch when we heard a heavy footfall on the stair, and the door opened to reveal the bulky figure of the saturnine Mycroft Holmes on the threshold.

"Mycroft! How pleasant to see you! Please take a seat. Would you care for a whisky?"

The older Holmes brother remained where he was.

"This isn't a social call, Sherlock, and while the matter affects you, it is chiefly to Dr. Watson that I wish to speak."

"Me?"

"Yes, sir, you. I am aware that you and my brother have recently concluded what you would no doubt term an 'adventure' concerning a certain substance that has a particular effect upon the human nervous system. No doubt you plan to publish an account of the business."

"Well, I was – "

"No such account must ever be written. Or, if written, it must never be published. Should you ever do so, I promise you that there will be consequences of a most serious nature."

The younger Holmes got to his feet.

"I will endure much from you, Mycroft, but when it comes to threatening Watson, that is something I will not tolerate."

Mycroft's expression softened a little.

"Your loyalty to your friend does you credit, Sherlock. But I must ask you both to seriously consider the results of making the existence of this drug known. As long as these 'walking dead', as one might call them, are considered fables, and confined to a small and inconsequential island, they represent no danger. Imagine, however, what might happen if the story is credited in the palaces and chancellories of the great foreign powers. Surely you can see that they would do everything they can to manufacture or obtain supplies of the mixture. I trust you wouldn't wish to see it fall into the hands of the Kaiser, or of the Sultan of Turkey."

"Very well," I said. "I accept your reasoning, and I will not send the story to be published."

"You have made a wise decision, sir."

"Goodbye, Brother. It was, as ever, a pleasure to see you."

"Sarcasm ill becomes you, Sherlock. Good day, gentlemen."

The Three Archers

Those who have followed my chronicles of the exploits of Mr. Sherlock Holmes from their earliest publication will be aware that the first of them, *A Study in Scarlet*, is described, in part, as being *"A Reprint from The Reminiscences of John H. Watson, M.D., Late of the Army Medical Department"*. This has led some of my readers to inquire if it is possible to also obtain a copy of that book. The answer, alas, is no.

Any aspiring author can tell the tale of his or her early frustrations: The return of one's manuscript by publisher after publisher, the loss of a book in transit, (making it necessary to choose between rewriting the entire story and abandoning the enterprise altogether), or acceptance of one's manuscript accompanied by a demand for drastic cutting or revision.

My *Reminiscences* fall into the last category. My publishers determined that the public would not be interested in the story of my upbringing, my schooldays, and my early visits to the United States and Australia, and that the narrative really begins with my meeting Holmes, the main interest being our pursuit and capture of Jefferson Hope. The second section, "The Country of the Saints", while it is based on the experiences of Hope and the Ferriers, contains a strong element of fiction, as I was required to concoct a narrative using the meagre information on the subject I had to hand.

So while *A Study in Scarlet* drew on my manuscript, it cannot truly be described as a "reprint", since the original was never printed, and so does not exist as a separate entity. No doubt the publishers thought that it made the narrative appear more authoritative. I must admit that in all probability, they made the right decision, although I did not believe that to be the case at the time.

Another point which correspondents frequently raise in connection with that first book is: Why does Holmes's practice seem to consist, in those early days, entirely of cases which he can solve without leaving the confines of 221b Baker Street? Was the Lauriston Gardens mystery the first time he solved a case by visiting the location of the crime and questioning witnesses?

Certainly, it was the first occasion on which he asked *me* to accompany him, but from conversations with him over many years it is clear that both the police and clients had summoned him to various locations during his time in Montague Street. It must also be remembered that during those first weeks during which we shared rooms, I was still in the last stages of a long convalescence, and thus unable in any event to accompany him on cases which demanded that he leave our lodgings.

As time went on, and Holmes's reputation grew, he could both command higher fees and be more selective about which cases in which he would become involved. The number which he could solve without leaving his armchair dwindled, but didn't disappear altogether. I have already related he stories of Mary Sutherland and her duplicitous stepfather, and that of John

Openshaw and the five orange pips. The following narrative takes place some years later, but falls into a similar category.

By the year 1896, the popularity of archery had gone a little into decline. It had been surpassed as a fashionable pastime for the middle classes by sports such as croquet and tennis. Nevertheless, some fifty archery clubs still remained in Britain. In 1894, the first Olympics committee, headed by Baron Pierre de Coubertin, announced that the 1900 Games would take place in Paris, and that archery would be among the events. This provoked a fierce atmosphere of competition among that group of practitioners who made up the members of the remaining clubs. The fact that six years must elapse before the British team was chosen seemed to have intensified that atmosphere rather than dissipated it.

The Fernfield Archery Club near High Barnet in north London was one of the oldest in the country, having been founded in 1863, only two years after the formation of the Grand National Archery Society. The GNAS organized the Annual National Championship competitions, and would also have a considerable say in who was chosen to represent the country in the first British Olympic archery team. Fernfield's reputation was good. Only two of its members had ever won the championship, but they were always well represented in the semi- and quarter-finals.

In the year 1896, the club had three outstanding archers: W.H. Cullen, D.N. Edginton, and R.H. McNeil. In June, the month before that year's championship, it appeared certain that one of them would win the competition, though it was difficult to say which, since they seemed equally adept. Under those circumstances, it was understandable that there was a great rivalry amongst them, but that rivalry took different forms in each of the three men, who had starkly contrasting personalities. Robert Hugh McNeil was the most popular of the three among the hundred or so members of the club. A sandy-haired Scot from Edinburgh, he was a lawyer who had moved his practice to London when he married a woman from Hampstead. Fond of a drink, but not to excess, he was easy-going, and while he trained hard, he wasn't obsessive. Archery came naturally to him – he was good at it – but he didn't allow it to interfere with the attention he paid to his wife and child. If Edginton or Cullen beat him, he would be disappointed, but no more.

Dennis Noel Edginton counted McNeil among his friends, and it was as if he saw in the affable Scot the image of what he would like to be, but felt he never could. He was moody and insecure and spent virtually all his free time on his sport. McNeil alone was able to coax him out of his bouts of sullenness with some amicable teasing and a few drinks in the club bar. If Robbie McNeil was the most amiable of the three, Walter Henry Cullen was the most disliked. He was a braggart, and continually sought to undermine his rivals with insults and sneering assertions as to their lack of skill. McNeil had no problem laughing this off, but Edginton's sensitive soul was mauled by it. On one occasion, after some drinks in the bar, Cullen went over to his table and whispered something in Edginton's ear which was so offensive –

no one ever discovered what it was – that Edginton stood and was about to take a swing at Cullen. McNeil restrained his friend, and surprised everyone by threatening to hit Cullen himself if he didn't leave.

Cullen's indisputable ability was the only thing that prevented the club committee from expelling him. Not long after he provoked Edginton, he tried to force his attentions on one of the club waitresses, and this, along with his general habit of treating them as grossly inferior, encouraged the entire catering staff to refuse to serve him unless he gave an apology. This was duly given, but thereafter Cullen stopped dining or drinking at the bar and restaurant. Any time he spent at the club was mostly occupied with archery.

A description of the club buildings is necessary at this point, based on photographs taken by the police. At the front of the clubhouse were two doors. The larger one, on the right, led into a hall leading to the reception room, while a smaller door on the left was to a room where equipment could be stored in personal lockers. This also contained small changing rooms for men and women members. Another door at the far end of the room opened onto the club restaurant, which could also be accessed by a side door.

Next to the restaurant was the bar, the only place where smoking was allowed. It was accessed by another door. Connecting to the bar, the restaurant, and the reception area was a large room which also contained the kitchen and a separate seating area for the staff. A door led into reception and, as part of the same wall, there was a space with a reception desk with a curtain behind it so that visitors couldn't see into the room.

The reception area had two windows, both of which looked out onto the large, square flat lawn to the right of the building where the practice of archery was actually carried out. The rest of the clubhouse consisted of two offices and a committee room which shared walls with the kitchen and the bar, but were only accessible by a door at the back of the building.

It was seven o'clock on the evening of June 16th, and because of the heat, many of the doors and windows, including those of the reception room, were fully open. Cullen, Edginton, and McNeil were the only members still out on the butts, and the other members who had been present that day, twenty in all, being either in the bar or at dinner. Cullen was the first to stop. He walked back to the clubhouse and went and sat in the reception area.

A few minutes later one of the staff went into reception and found Cullen dead, lying down with an arrow sticking in the nape of his neck. He kept his head and left the corpse, and the scene, untouched, and then went into the restaurant via the kitchen and informed the Club Treasurer, Mr. Lionel Harris, what he had found. Harris instantly went 'round into his office and telephoned the local constabulary, who, as was common in murder cases, notified Scotland Yard. He then had the main door to the club locked and allowed the rest of the members to finish their meals and drinks (the club closed at nine), and leave. He was later criticised for this action, but defended himself on the grounds that he had been in the restaurant and had seen no one leave.

The door to the bar had been closed, but he knew there were only three people in there and none had passed by the open restaurant windows. His immediate concern had been to neither upset nor panic the members, particularly the female ones. As McNeil had only just come into the restaurant, Harris told him to remain. He asked him if there was anyone else on the butts. McNeil replied that Cullen had just come off but Edginton was either still out there or in the locker room. Edginton had in fact gone into the reception area, and was there when the door was locked as per Harris's instructions.

When the police arrived, Edginton was seated in a chair, gazing down at his rival's corpse with an unfathomable expression. He was still dressed as he had been at the butts and had his bow and arrows. Inspector Stanley Hopkins of Scotland Yard arrived at about half-past-nine, accompanied by the medical examiner, a sergeant, and a police photographer. Hopkins apologised for his late arrival. The examiner, Dr. James Cardew, had been delayed by another murder in Camden Town and none of his colleagues had been available.

The site of the murder was photographed from several angles. Cardew then confirmed that Cullen's death was caused by the arrow in the back of his neck, and that death would have occurred instantaneously, or within two or three seconds at most, and had taken place in the last two to two-and-a-half hours. Hopkins then questioned McNeil, Edginton, and Huggins, the man who had discovered the body, in the Treasurer's office. Notes were taken in shorthand by Sergeant Griffiths.

These were the facts, as they were presented to us by Inspector Hopkins one evening as we sat with the Scotland Yarder in our rooms in Baker Street

"And what did those three gentlemen have to say for themselves?" asked Sherlock Holmes, leaning forward, the expression on his sharp features akin to that of the hound who catches the far-off scent of the fox.

The case had reached an impasse, so the inspector had swallowed his pride and come to ask for assistance from the one man in London who could help him with his investigation.

"McNeil says the three of them – that is, himself, Cullen, and Edginton – were out at the butts for about two hours. Cullen left first. McNeil was going to keep Edginton company, but decided to go to the restaurant and get something to eat."

"Did McNeil see Cullen in the reception area?" asked Holmes.

"He said that the door was open and Cullen was sitting in a chair about halfway between the door and the reception desk."

"Why did he go into the reception area rather than the restaurant?"

"He hadn't been in the bar or restaurant for a while, but he was prepared to pay a bit extra for someone to bring him a drink there. Apparently he would have one or two on his own there, and then get changed and leave."

"So, what did McNeil do after he saw Cullen?"

"He says he went and changed his clothes, put his bow and arrows away, then went into the restaurant. He ordered a meal, but before it arrived Mr. Harris asked him to stay after the club closed. He didn't find out why until we arrived. He took his time over his meal and then went into the bar, where he had a couple of drinks and read the newspapers."

"Did you ask him if he saw Edginton at any point after leaving the butts?"

"He said he hadn't. When I asked him if he had got on with the dead man, he admitted that Cullen was a first-class archer, but he was too arrogant about it, and that if he were honest, he wouldn't miss him.

"I let McNeil go and spoke to Edginton. He said the last time he had seen Cullen alive was when McNeil was leaving the butts to get something to eat. Edginton turned to tell McNeil he'd join him in a little while, and saw Cullen sitting in an armchair near the reception desk. Both windows were open, and he saw him through the right-hand one. That was about thirty yards from where he was standing."

"And Edginton was sure it was him?"

"So he said. Edginton then stayed and took a few more shots, gathered his arrows, and started for the clubhouse. When he got to the main door, he looked in and saw someone lying on the floor with an arrow in his neck. He went along the hall and saw it was Cullen.

"I asked him why he had stayed there, and he said he needed to sit down because he was in shock. There was no one else in the room. I was told later that Huggins had already discovered the body, and informed Mr. Harris before Edginton claims to have seen it. Then one of the staff locked the main door, not realizing that Edginton was in there, as the whole of the reception area isn't visible from the door. It was unlocked when we arrived. McNeil took Edginton to the bar and went behind it and got him a drink. Edginton admitted that plenty of the members had a motive for killing Cullen, but that he was high on the list. He denied being the murderer, but I felt he was uncomfortable because by saying he hadn't done it, he might be incriminating his friend.

"The last to be interviewed was Huggins, the staff member who had found Cullen. He was a virtual giant of a man, and I had to remind myself that the idea that big strong men were lacking in intellect was a dangerous cliche. Huggins's face displayed little emotion, but there was intelligence in those brown eyes.

"He stated that he had been working at the club for seven years. He was a little reluctant at first to give his opinion of Cullen, but when pressed described him as 'a bad'un', and said they should've kicked him out when he tried it on with Sarah – that was the waitress he had insulted – and would have been, if it wasn't for the National Championships and "their precious Olympics". He had joined the rest of the staff when they boycotted Cullen. According to Mr. McNeil, one of the staff was supplying him with drinks in the reception room for an inflated price. I asked Huggins if he had any idea who that might be.

"Huggins squirmed in his chair, a strange movement for so large a man, and admitted that it was him.

"'Money is money, sir,' he said. 'A bit extra always comes in handy. Please don't tell the committee, sir. I won't do it again. I mean, I can't do it again now, can I? Not now he's dead.'

"'All right, we'll pass over that,' I said. 'Just tell me what happened.'

"There wasn't much to tell. Cullen came in and rang the reception bell. Huggins went and answered it, and when Cullen saw it was him, he ordered a drink. Huggins went to get it, and when he came back, there Cullen was, dead, with that arrow sticking out of his neck. Huggins went for Mr. Harris, and the rest is as I have said."

"What do you make of it, then, Hopkins?" Holmes asked.

"Well, sir, it has to be either Edginton or McNeil, doesn't it? Both were excellent with the bow, and both hated Cullen. Ezdginton could have shot him through the open window, and McNeil could have stood at the open door and shot an arrow along the length of the hall into the reception room. It's a question of deciding which one. Edginton seems too nervous and sensitive to have done it, and McNeil seems too amiable – at first glance, anyway. We all know from experience that everyone has hidden depths, and that murder can find a home in what seems the softest of hearts."

"True," I said.

"It doesn't seem premeditated," Hopkins continued. "Edginton could have simply given in to a sudden impulse, and what we saw wasn't simply shock, but genuine remorse, and maybe horror at discovering that he was capable of murder. He doesn't seem the type who can live with guilt for any length of time. As to McNeil, Harris told us that McNeil uncharacteristically threatened Cullen when Cullen insulted Edginton. Was his friendship for Edginton so great that he'd kill to get Cullen off his friend's back?"

"You could look at it from a different angle," I said. "From what you've told us, McNeil and Cullen were polar opposites. They were bound to come into conflict."

"To the point of murder? And again, it seems unpremeditated, so we fall back on the idea that it was the result of a momentary impulse. McNeil saw Cullen, he had the weapons to hand, and *Whoosh!* Cullen's dead. McNeil then acted with fantastic coolness, went to his locker, got changed, and strolled into the restaurant, ordered a meal, and showed no sign of stress when Harris asked him to stay after the club closed."

"While these speculations are interesting, and no doubt of importance," said Holmes, "let us look first at what facts we have. Was the type of the arrow that killed Cullen the same as those used by Edginton or McNeil?"

"That was one of the first things I thought of, Mr. Holmes. Unfortunately, it is of the most common make, which is used by virtually everyone in the club."

"What was the exact position of the body when it was found?"

Hopkins reached into a small briefcase he had brought with him and produced a manila folder.

"These are the photographs of the murder scene, taken by our man, Atkinson. He's very thorough, and took them from every possible point of view."

The pictures showed a dark-haired man of middle height, in his early thirties, dressed in archery gear, on his face on the floor with his head pointing in the direction of the door and the fatal arrow protruding from his neck. His bow and quiver of arrows lay on a chair.

"What do you make of them, Watson?" asked Holmes.

"I'm afraid these give no indication of the direction the arrow came from. As Cardew said, death would have been virtually instantaneous, but that doesn't mean that in his last moment Cullen's body might not have twisted, either in agony or from the force of the blow."

Holmes leafed through the photographs and after a minute or so gave a little smile of triumph.

"Nevertheless, gentlemen, these give us clear pointers as to the identity of the murderer."

"Then who should I arrest – Edginton or McNeil?"

"Neither. Your culprit, Inspector, is Huggins."

"Huggins? But he reported the crime!"

"Of course he reported it. Suspicion would have instantly fallen on him if he hadn't. As an intelligent man, he would have realized that."

"But the murder must have been committed by an archer, and Huggins was a member of the staff, not of the club."

"Really, my friend, you must learn to look at the facts, and not rely upon your assumptions. Just because the man was killed by an arrow, that doesn't necessarily mean that it was shot from a bow."

Holmes spread the photographs across the small table around which we were sitting. I picked up each one and scrutinised it, but could find nothing to support Holmes's assertions.

"Our first indication that Huggins was lying can be clearly seen," began Holmes. "Or rather, clearly *not* seen. No?" he continued after a few seconds. "You still don't understand? According to Huggins, Cullen ordered a drink. Huggins went to fetch it, and when he returned, found Cullen dead and instantly went to inform Harris, who had the door closed. Where, then, is the drink? Had Huggins really brought one in, he would have put it down somewhere before going to tell Harris. But it is nowhere to be seen.

"Our second and third points may both be inferred from the arrow wound. Any arrow fired from a bow would have had sufficient force to not merely enter the back of the neck, but to go right through it. Then there is the angle of the wound. Again, if fired from a bow, it would enter at an angle of ninety degrees. The angle here is closer to forty-five degrees, which is consistent with the arrow being stabbed down *into* the neck by someone somewhat taller than the victim, and possessed of considerable strength.

"So, Cullen comes into the reception area, puts his bow and quiver on the nearest chair and rings the reception bell. When Huggins appears, he orders a drink and then turns his back, Huggins takes one of the arrows from the quiver and stabs it downwards into Cullen's neck."

"That's all very neat and logical, Mr. Holmes, but why did Huggins do it? He needed the extra money he made from supplying Cullen with drinks."

"From what you've said, Huggins is a large, powerful man. In my experience, such men may be divided into two broad categories. There are those who use their strength unscrupulously to gain whatever may be achieved by it, and those who have been taught from an early age, usually by their mothers, that their strength must be used carefully and responsibly, particularly where the weak are concerned. As the weaker sex, women are especially to be protected. As a manifestation of this tendency, consider how often one sees large men married to much smaller women.

"Yes, Huggins was dependent on Cullen for extra money. But he was also aware that Cullen had mistreated Sarah, for whom it is possible that Huggins has paternal, or even romantic, feelings. He may have loathed himself for accepting payment from such a man. These passions warred within him until – in one moment – he snapped. Casting self-restraint aside, he seized the nearest weapon to hand and dealt the fatal blow. I also think it entirely possible that had you arrested either Edginton or McNeil, Huggins would have come forward and confessed."

Hopkins stood up.

"Well, I shall certainly arrest him, and we shall see whether your speculations are correct. Thank you, Mr. Holmes. A very nice piece of work."

Huggins was tried at the Old Bailey some weeks later, and Holmes's theories turned out to be true in every particular. Among the witnesses was Sarah Crowden, a petite young woman who testified that she was sure that Huggins was in love with her, but hadn't spoken due to the twenty-five-year difference in age between them.

The jury found Huggins guilty after a very brief consultation, but submitted a recommendation for mercy, the mitigating circumstances being Huggins' previous good character, the bad character of the victim, exemplified by his mistreatment of the girl, and the fact that the act hadn't been premeditated. The judge concurred, and gave Huggins a custodial sentence with the possibility of parole, instead of sending him to the gallows.

The Adventure of the Long Arm

It was, I remember, towards the end of a particularly windy afternoon in late autumn when Holmes received a note from Inspector Lestrade of Scotland Yard. Through the windows of our rooms in Baker Street, one could see the fallen leaves and other items of urban detritus whirling along the darkening thoroughfare, while folk hurried along the pavement, clasping their outer garments to them against the rising cold. For my own part, I would have been perfectly content to remain by our fire, consulting my notebook, and composing the latest addition to my already copious collection of narratives concerning my experiences in the company of my celebrated fellow-lodger. The message from Lestrade, however, specifically requested my presence as well as that of Mr. Sherlock Holmes.

Of late, Holmes had become interested in the history of firearms, and as well as reading as many texts on the subject as he could accumulate. He was also experimenting with gunpowder, mixing it up from charcoal, sulfur, and saltpeter. This didn't make for a particularly pleasing atmosphere, but I was always happy to see him involved in any of his various interests, for while he was concentrated on these pursuits, he was distracted from any lack of cases, and therefore less likely to succumb to the temptation of resorting to any form of chemical stimulus. It was true that he had not used cocaine for many months, but the possibility that he might revert to its consumption was always there, an omnipresent spectre at the feast.

When he had read Lestrade's note, he rose from the seat at the acid-scarred deal table and strode towards the door. He took both our overcoats from their hooks and held mine out at arm's length.

"Come along," he said in a commanding tone. "The good inspector has summoned us both."

I reluctantly set my notebook and pencil to one side and pulled my coat from his bony hand.

"We'll miss dinner," I said somewhat petulantly.

"I'm sure Mrs. Hudson will gladly provide us with something when we return. Who knows – perhaps Lestrade will have a case for us which will be worthy of inclusion in your memoirs. You wouldn't want to miss that on account of your stomach, would you?"

I said nothing, but put on my overcoat with a sigh and followed his lithe figure as he eagerly hurried down the stairs and pulled open the front door. Fortunately we didn't have long to wait before the appearance of an empty hansom for hire.

When we arrived at Scotland Yard, the desk sergeant recognised us and informed us that Inspector Lestrade was waiting down in the police mortuary. We descended a set of metal steps and went along the familiar dingy corridor and through a set of double doors into a large room full of long tables whose walls were covered in cold, pale-green tiles.

A single body lay on one of the tables under a voluminous white sheet. Next to it was the familiar face and wiry little form of the Scotland Yarder.

"Good evening, gentlemen," he said. "I'm glad you could come."

"You've asked us here to look at a body?" I said. "Surely you have your own police surgeons for that."

"Of course, Doctor, and one of them will be taking a look at it. But once you've seen it, you'll understand why I've called on you and Mr. Holmes. But I warn you: It isn't a pretty sight."

"We've both seen plenty of the dead," Holmes remarked. "What makes this one so special?"

"See for yourself," said Lestrade, pulling away the sheet. It was a man's body, naked, though perhaps that was to be expected, given where it was. What was unexpected was that the head, hands, and feet had all been removed. Not only the spirit, or the life force, or whatever name one cared to give to the animating principle, was gone, but so too were the indicators of identity that preserved whatever remained of individuality, of personality, leaving only a slab of meat. It was, as Lestrade had indicated, unsettling.

"The only thing we can be sure of," the policeman said with a wry smile, "is his religion."

"Why, because he's circumcised?" said Holmes. "My dear Lestrade, you should know better than that. More than one religion practices circumcision, though I grant you that the balance of probability is against his being a Muslim. There aren't too many of them in London, and the paleness of his skin means he's less likely to be an Arab. And don't forget, some people have it done to their sons on medical grounds."

Holmes took his magnifying glass from the pocket of his Inverness and bent over to examine the organ in question. "I think he was, indeed, a recent convert to the Jewish religion," he said after a few seconds, straightening up, "and that he was engaged to be married. Do you concur, Watson?" he asked, handing me his glass.

"I agree with the first part," I said, when I had taken a look, "but I don't see how you arrive at the second."

"The scarring has not fully healed, which means the operation was carried out in the last six to eight weeks."

"That much is certainly correct."

"While the surgical process is perfectly safe, it is still not something most adult males would happily undergo. So he had a strong reason for wanting it performed. What is the strongest reason there could be? Love, the most common factor in religious conversions. He met a woman of the Jewish faith, fell in love with her, and demonstrated the seriousness of his intentions, and his conversion, by having his foreskin removed. At the same time, he would not have done so if he was not assured that she returned his feelings. So I infer that they were engaged, shortly before or shortly after."

"Engaged? How do you know he didn't have it done after they were married?" asked Lestrade.

"Intercourse isn't possible until after it's fully healed. Which, as Watson confirmed, takes about six to eight weeks. Now, while most people are prepared to wait out their engagement, few would be ready to go for that amount of time without being able to consummate their marriage."

"That sounds logical enough," said Lestrade.

"It's a working hypothesis, at least," said Holmes. "Was he found like this, without clothes?"

"Yes."

"That deprives us of one set of clues. Where was he found?"

"Morgan Street, a nasty little back-street in Whitechapel. A nine-year-old girl found him early this morning. Scared the living daylights out of her, poor little thing."

"Let us turn to the rest of his body. What do you make of it, Watson?"

The first thing that met my eye was a series of odd circular wounds that were scattered across the chest, belly, and legs of the victim. They could not be accidental. They must be intentional.

"This man has been tortured," I said.

"Burnt with a cigarette or cigar, " said Holmes. "Nothing else would produce such marks. He worked in the open air, either in short sleeves or with long sleeves rolled up. Though the tan has faded a little due to the time of year, it is still visible, extending from just above the elbow down to the wrists. Whatever labour he was engaged in, it was not hard physical labour. The body is generally fit, but the muscles in his arms are not particularly developed. He spent a lot of time kneeling."

Holmes pointed to the slight but noticeable callosities on the knees.

He pulled out his glass once more, this time looking at the neck, wrists, and ankles.

"At least two people carried out the amputations. The cuts that took off the hands and feet are clean, but the incisions on the neck are ragged. All were probably done with a heavy meat cleaver. A strong man might be able to cut through the wrists and ankles with one blow each. A skillful man might need two, but could still do it cleanly. Whoever cut the neck hacked at it with several blows before the head came off. I hope for this poor devil's sake that wasn't what actually killed him. If his head was in proportion to his body, he must have been about five feet six."

"One thing I don't see is why they cut his feet off," said Lestrade. "I mean, the head and hands I can understand, but you can't identify someone by their feet. Unless – unless he had some sort of deformity or birthmark on one of them. But then, why cut off both?"

"Well," said Holmes, "if you only cut off one, you draw attention to the fact that there may have been something distinctive about it. But I'm not entirely convinced that the purpose of the amputations was the concealment of this man's identity. In fact, I believe I can identify him. Has anything struck you, Watson?"

"I cannot say that it has."

"Let me help. Here we have a man who works in the open air, spends time on his knees, and rolls his sleeves up. That suggest that he is, or rather was, a gardener. He was engaged to be married to a Jewish woman . . . ."

I suddenly grasped who Holmes was describing.

"Good God!" I cried. " Luigi Manoli!"

We had first heard the name some two weeks before, when Hannah Goldman called on us one morning at Baker Street.

She was a petite young woman with a pale face, dominated by a pair of large and beautiful brown eyes. Little wisps of dark wavy hair had escaped from the blue silk shawl that covered her head, which was the only spot of colour in her clothes, the rest being plain black and clearly of poor quality.

The morning was chilly, and when Mrs. Hudson saw the young lady's pallor, she insisted on bringing her a hot bowl of beef broth, which Miss Goldman consumed gratefully. When she had set the bowl aside, Holmes inquired how we might be of service.

"It is my fiancé, Luigi Manoli, Mr. Holmes. We are due to be married soon, but he has vanished."

"How long have you known him, Miss Goldman?"

"About ten months. We have been engaged for three. I first met him when he was walking out with my friend, Sarah Wilkins, but when he saw me, and I saw him, there was an instant attraction, and before too long it had deepened into love."

She lowered her eyes and added, "The first love I have known."

Holmes pressed his hands together before him and said, "And how did Sarah Wilkins react to this development?"

"She was happy for me, happy for both of us. She liked Luigi, of course, but she had not been serious about him. She is my friend. She would not steal him from me, if that is what you were thinking."

As she spoke these words, I saw a hint of a fiery spirit within that slender body and behind that pale face.

"Are there any other young women in his life?"

"No. I have already said – He loves me."

"Then tell us about Luigi," said Holmes. "Does he have any enemies?"

"No, no. He is a good man, a gentle man. He is a gardener for the City of London, he loves to plant things, to watch them grow. He has no hatred in his heart for anyone."

"Was he born in London?"

"No, he came on the boat from Italy, about five years ago."

"From where in Italy, exactly?"

"I don't know. I have never asked. He has never told me anything about his life before he came to England."

"Are you not at least curious?" I interjected.

"Yes, but I am also in love. I know all I need to know – that he is a good man, that he truly loves me, and I him. If he wanted to tell me about his former life, I would listen, but if he does not want to, I will not pry."

Holmes stood.

"Miss Goldman, I am not without sympathy for your plight, but there is little I can do without more data. Do you have a photograph of your fiancée?"

"Yes, yes."

She reached into the pocket of her coat and pulled out a picture.

"Then I suggest you take it to Scotland Yard, or the police station nearest Mr. Manoli's residence, and ask them to deal with the matter."

Hannah Goldman pushed herself up from her chair and said, "So, I will get no help from the great Mr. Sherlock Holmes! I was told that you were willing to help poor people who came to you with their troubles, but it seems that is wrong."

Holmes remained calm.

"I assure you, Miss Goldman, that the wealth or poverty of those who come to consult me is of no importance. It is simply that in your particular case, there is little I can do on the basis of the information you have given me. In such a matter, the official force has more resources than I do. However, I will make a promise: If you leave your address, then should I gain any information at all about your fiancé, I will inform you of the fact. That really is, at the moment, the best I can do."

"Luigi Manoli!" echoed Lestrade. "I remember the name. He's on the missing list. His fiancée came and reported it. Rather pretty, she was. What was her name?"

"Hannah Goldman," I answered. "And yes, she's pretty. Beautiful, even."

I had seen the address on the piece of paper the young woman had handed Holmes. Like Morgan Street where the body was discovered, it was one of the poorest in the East End. If that was all she could afford, then she was doubtless working in one of the worst-paid jobs – as a match girl, perhaps, or as a seamstress in a garment factory. How long would that prettiness, and that spirit, survive the long hours of hard work, the years of poverty, and the childbearing that probably lay in her future? Childbearing, if – when she had recovered from the grief of losing Manoli – she was lucky enough to find another man who loved her. But of that, there could be no guarantee. Two lines from Chaucer floated into my mind:

O scatheful harm, condition of poverty,
With thirst, with cold, with hunger so confounded.

"Well," Lestrade was saying, "she must be told, though it's a task anyone on the Force would avoid if he could. Although thinking about it, we can't, in the absence of clear identifying factors, be one-hundred-per-cent sure that this is Manoli's body, can we?"

"I agree that the evidence isn't conclusive," said Holmes, "but the overwhelming probability is that the body is Manoli's. If it is not, and there is an innocent reason for Manoli's absence, he will return, and in her joy Miss Goldman will forgive the police for any grief you have brought her. If he is still alive, and has vanished because he's with another woman, or has fled after committing a crime, then she is well rid of him, and it is better that she thinks him dead."

"That's certainly one way of looking at it, I suppose," agreed Lestrade. "Well, thank you for coming, Mr. Holmes, Dr. Watson."

"Send us a copy of the Police Surgeon's report."

"Certainly. Good evening, gentlemen."

The solemnity of the experience had made me forget the state of my appetite, but, as Holmes had predicted, when we returned to Baker Street, Mrs. Hudson had already begun heating up some food in anticipation of our arrival. I gladly fell to it, but Holmes sat with his plate untouched, a faraway look in his keen grey eyes. He remained silent for the next two hours, and I went to bed, leaving him in his accustomed armchair with the smoke from his pipe curling above his head.

As Lestrade had promised, we received a copy of the medical report the following day. In a note at the bottom of the final page, the inspector added that no one else on the list of missing persons resembled the description of the body, and he was therefore convinced that it must be Manoli.

The Police Surgeon confirmed that the amount of blood remaining in the body meant that the amputations had been carried out after death. Neither the contents of the stomach nor the blood contained any trace of poison. The surgeon concluded that death might have been caused by strangulation, whether by hand or by ligature, or the throat slit. The ragged state of the neck wounds would serve to conceal either of those methods. Another likely possibility was that the victim had died from a blow to the head.

Holmes summoned Billy, scribbled something on a page torn from one of his notebooks, and told the lad to take it to Scotland Yard. The boy returned in about three-quarters-of-an-hour with another piece of paper on which was written: "*No. 8*".

"*No. 8?*"

"The number of the house in Morgan Street in front of which the little girl found Manoli's corpse. That, Watson, is where we are going this evening. I trust that your old army revolver is in good working order."

"You saw me clean it only the other day."

"So I did. Well, need I add, load it and bring it with you tonight."

With that old familiar thrill of adventure coursing through my being, I joined Holmes as he summoned a cab. When were inside, he yelled to the driver, "Aldgate!"

I gave him a puzzled look.

"Aldgate? But Morgan Street is in Whitechapel, so why Aldgate?"

"As you know, my friend, I keep several rented rooms throughout the metropolis in which I can change both my clothes and my appearance. I keep one in Aldgate because, while it is close enough to the East End to be accessible on foot, it is also too far from there for any of the East End's denizens to see me enter as my own self and leave as someone else. Believe me, if someone suspected that Sherlock Holmes was walking the streets of Whitechapel, and saw me depart in my disguise, my life would not have an hour's purchase."

"But I am with you, and while I'm not as easily recognized as you, it will surely give the game away if I'm at your side."

Holmes gave a little chuckle.

"Really, Watson! What would you suggest?"

"You mean, I am also to be in disguise? But I have no talent for such play-acting. And – you don't intend to have me shave off my moustache?"

"Certainly not. From the many times you have seen me in the guise of someone else, you must have realised that a mere change of clothing is often enough."

"Well, perhaps, but I still say that to be truly effective, the man in disguise must be something of an actor."

"All you need do is remain silent, and leave any talking that may need to be done to me."

Never before had I been in one of Holmes's secret rooms, so I was full of curiosity when we entered an unprepossessing building a street away from the Aldgate pump. Some of the windows were boarded over, and the paint of the front door was almost completely peeled away. Holmes took out a key and turned it in the lock, and as we entered the small hallway, I noticed a distinct, musty smell in the air. As we climbed the somewhat rickety stairs, I saw no sign that the place had any other inhabitants. Whoever owned it was probably glad that there was someone paying some rent, and Holmes was no doubt handing over more than the market price, which would not be difficult. We entered a room on the first floor. Holmes lit a gas lamp, illuminating a chamber that was purely functional, with no sign of any creature comforts. There was a bed, and if for any reason Holmes had to spend a night there, it would just about accommodate his long frame.

Holmes opened a large mahogany wardrobe. Inside was a variety of clothes, hats, and shoes, and on the floor of the cabinet there was a large wooden box full of wigs, false moustaches, and beards, and other less-immediately recognisable elements of disguise.

"We'll set you up first," said Holmes with a smile, and pulled out an off-white shirt that had seen better days, a thoroughly disreputable topcoat, dingy and threadbare, and a pair of brown trousers that were visibly thin at the knee. I divested myself of my respectable outfit and donned those uninviting garments, hoping as I did so that none of them were inhabited by fleas.

"Try on some of the shoes, " said Holmes, as began removing his own clothes. "There should be a pair there that will fit you."

At last, we stood facing each other. Holmes was clad in an old sailor's jacket, a pair of faded khaki trousers that must once have belonged to a soldier, and a collarless undershirt. He put a grubby knee-length coat over this ensemble and regarded me.

"You look splendid, Watson."

There was no mirror for me to look at myself in, but I strongly doubted that "splendid" was the *mot juste* for my appearance.

"Now, we just need a few finishing touches."

He rammed a dark curly wig on my head, then glued a pair of side-whiskers to his face and took out two hats, one a dusty bowler which he placed on his own head, the other, a battered cap, he handed to me.

"Left!" cried Holmes when we were once more out in the street. The weather was still somewhat chilly, though the wind had died down. I have never been a frequenter of the East End, and I was worried at first that Holmes had overdone our disguises. But as we made our way through Shoreditch and into Whitechapel, I became aware that many of the passers-by were dressed in clothes that were easily as down-at-heel and mismatched as those we were wearing. Nevertheless, I was happy that I could feel the weight of my old army revolver in the pocket of my shabby coat.

After about twenty minutes' walk we reached our destination in Morgan Street. It was an ill-lit, narrow street along which stretched a line of houses which were, by the area's standards, in reasonably good condition, but were identically dull and monotonous, built merely for use and function. Unlike the main streets along which we had passed, which were full of pedestrians in the middle of the evening, in this back alley there was no one to be seen.

"Now," said Holmes," we need to speak to the inhabitant of No. 8, but I rather suspect he will not open the door to us, not even a crack to see who we are."

"Why not?"

"Because he is in fear for his life. Unless I am much mistaken, he is a fugitive from his own land, and his whereabouts have been the subject of speculation in the European press.'"

"What should we do, then?"

"Observe, Watson, that there is only one light burning in the whole house, on the first floor. That must be where he is. Now, we shall go around to the back of the house, climb over the wall that runs along all the yards in the street, and effect an entry on the ground floor."

So once more, we were breaking the law. I had to trust, from my past experiences with Holmes, that this departure from the straight-and-narrow would have an outcome that would justify our transgression.

Within minutes we were over the wall and standing before a ground floor window. From his shabby coat, my companion drew his glass-cutter and removed a half-circle from the window, next to the handle, then reached inside and turned it. As silently as we could, we crept through the house and up the stairs, and along a short corridor until we saw a light under one of the doors.

Holmes signalled that I should stand by the wall on the right of the door, while he took the left side.

"Count Ridolfi!" he cried. "We have come to help you!"

"So you come for me at last!" came the answer in perfect English, spoken with a recognisably Italian accent. Then there were two loud bursts of gunfire, and the air sang with shattered shards of wood as two bullets ripped through the wooden door.

"I am Sherlock Holmes, and you have surely heard of me. My friend, Doctor Watson, and I mean you no harm. Please allow us to come in."

He pulled off the false side-whiskers and gestured that I should remove the dark curly wig.

"Yes, I have heard of Holmes, but how do I know you are truly he?" the Count responded.

"Have you seen my picture?"

"Yes, but that means nothing."

"Let me open the door."

"Very well, but I warn you, if you or your friend make one false move, I will shoot you without mercy."

Holmes opened the door to reveal a man of about sixty, seated in an old wooden chair, his long legs stretched out before him. His whitening hair was brushed back from his broad, intellectual forehead, and his blue eyes, filled with suspicion, were nevertheless clear and bright. But his complexion was pallid, and his face bore clear signs of illness or stress.

"Are you armed?" he demanded. "Tell me the truth, and remember: There are still four bullets in my revolver."

"Yes," said Holmes.

"Then take out your guns, slowly, and drop them on the floor."

We complied.

Count Ridolfi's weapon remained trained on us.

"Now", he said. "Prove you are who you say you are."

"You are Count Giuseppe Ridolfi, former governor of the Italian province of Frascillata. You are a just and honourable man, and you ruled that backward part of the country as well as any man has. But your justice, and your fair dealings, made you a target for the *Vecchia Fratellanza* – in English, 'The Old Brotherhood'."

"Who are they?" I could not help asking.

"Well, Dr. Watson – if that is truly who you are – you have no doubt heard of the *Mafia*, from Sicily – "

"Yes."

" – and perhaps even the *Ndrangheta* of Calabria, and the *Camorra* of Naples."

"No, never."

"The southern part of Italy, along with the island of Sicily, has a long history of brigandage, of secret societies and social unrest. It is not surprising. It is a poor, agricultural area, and its economic weakness and political instability have often been exploited, both by foreign states and by the rest of the country. It is entirely understandable that in the past, before the unification, poor men banded together in their own interest, and that, when they had no access to justice and the law was loaded against them, they broke the law in the cause of justice. That they came together in secrecy, swore oaths of allegiance, and brought vengeance down on those who betrayed them. Inevitably, the original ideals gradually fell away and were replaced by the baser desires of tyranny and greed. And so it was with the *Vecchia Fratellanza*."

"And now," said Holmes, "you are threatened by the *Bracchio Lungo* – 'The Long Arm' – an elite band of assassins, chosen by the council of the Old Brotherhood for their skill in murder. Have you ever known them to employ Englishmen to carry out their work?"

"No, they would never do that. It would be a slur on what they are pleased to call their "honour". Very well, I shall trust you, and I hope it is not the last decision I make in my life."

He laid the revolver in his lap.

"Tell me, Mr. Holmes, how you came to know of this."

"A man was found outside this house. His head, his hands, and his feet had been cut off. Now, although my dealings with them have been few, I have made a study of the practices of these secret societies. I recognised the condition of the dead as a kind of message – a warning to a man pursued by the *Bracchio Lungo* that they know where he is and will soon wreak vengeance on him."

"And this is how they carry out the sentence," said Ridolfi. "The victim is held down and his head beaten to a bloody pulp. Then the head is cut off, along with the hands and feet. The purpose of these mutilations is to send a message – that he who betrays the brotherhood, or leaves it, or stands in its way, is not merely dead, but stripped of all identity, as if he never was. These animals call themselves *Christians*, but this is part of an ancient belief, from centuries before the word of God came to Italy, that if any part of a man's body cannot be found when he is buried, then he cannot attain the afterlife."

"The man who was murdered was Luigi Manoli," I said. "Did you know him?"

The Count passed one of his slender hands before his eyes.

"*Mio Dio!*" he exclaimed. "*Manoli!*"

"Who was he?"

"His father was high up in the Brotherhood, but his mother left him shortly after Luigi was born, and, repelled by his ways, took the boy to the far north of Italy, where she hoped to raise him free from his father's influence. But the older Manoli set the Long Arm upon her, and though it took them seven years, eventually they found Luigi and his mother in the small village near Lake Maggiore, where they had taken refuge. The mother was murdered while the boy was sleeping, and they took him back to Frascillata and handed him over to his father.

"As the son of a member of the high council, he might have risen high in the Brotherhood, but his mother, though long dead, had done her work well, and at the age of twenty he came to me and gave me all the information he thought I needed to bring down the Brotherhood. Though we were able to eliminate many of their cells, it became clear that we had not succeeded in wiping them out completely. It was then that I realised that Luigi was in great danger, and I had him carefully guarded until I could send him to England, where I believed he would be safe."

He cast down his eyes and murmured, "But I see I was wrong. The Long Arm pursued him, even as it pursues me."

He looked up.

"Do you know what some call me in *Frascillata*? They call me *Guiseppe Fortunato* – 'Lucky Giuseppe' – because I survived four of the Brotherhood's assassination attempts."

He smiled bitterly.

"In the first of those attempts, my son died from a bullet that was aimed at me, and in the third my wife was killed by a bomb they planted on our *terrazza*. How then, am I 'Lucky Giuseppe'? It is true, I escaped to London. I changed my appearance, shaving off my beard and moustache. My English is good enough to get by, but I have kept myself to myself and been as inconspicuous as I could. But still they have found me, and I ask myself: What do I have to live for, now that I have lost my family? The only answer I have is that when they finally come for me, I will take as many of them with me as I can."

I was dumbstruck by the sheer tragedy of this narration, but Holmes, as usual, was all business.

"Count Ridolfi, we are here because I know from my studies that the dumping of Manoli's body on your doorstep means that you have three days grace before they come for you. That is why we are here: To stand with you when that moment comes. Are you with me, Watson?"

Stirred as I was by the old count's story, and knowing that I would never leave Holmes's side when he was in danger, I could only answer, "Yes."

"Please leave, gentlemen. I cannot ask you to die on my behalf."

"They will not be expecting three of us to be here instead of only one", said Holmes. "That will give us an advantage."

"They usually operate in cells of six," said the Count, "so they will outnumber us two to one."

"I would also suggest that you turn off the gas light and burn a single candle, so that it will not be so obvious, at least from the street, which room we are occupying."

This was not the first time I had sat in a darkened room with Holmes, my revolver in my hand, awaiting the arrival of a man of violence. Or *men* of violence, in this case.

The crisis came in the early hours of the morning, when the sky was at its darkest and the world at its stillest. All sensible men were long abed. I counted myself a sensible man, yet here I was, awake, with every fibre of my being taut with anticipation of the conflict to come.

From the floor below us we heard the sound of a window being smashed.

"Their entry was somewhat less subtle than yours," the Count said wryly.

There came the sound of doors being slammed one by one, and I realised that the assassins were checking each room. My grip tightened on my revolver as I heard them climbing the stairs. Again, we heard them opening and closing doors, until I realised that the room in which we sat was the only one remaining unchecked. There was no light in the corridor, or they might have noticed the bullet holes in the door. They must have realised that they had reached their goal, but instead of them bursting into the room, guns blazing, there came through the door the sound of low muttering, too low for even the Italian count to make out what they were saying. For long moments nothing happened, and then, finally, the door was kicked open and by the flickering light of the candle I saw three of the ruffians enter.

Holmes and the Count instantly fired, taking two of them down, but I was distracted by a movement at the window. I whirled and saw the other three men in the act of raising their guns to fire at us through the pane. They must have brought some kind of ladder with them. Two bullets whizzed past either side of my head, but I stood my ground and fired off four rounds in rapid succession. I had clearly hit at least one of them, for he fell back with a cry, knocking one of his fellows down to the ground beside him. The last, taking in the situation at a glance, fired off a shot at the Count, who gave a sharp cry as the bullet penetrated his shoulder and fell to the floor.

I discharged my remaining two rounds at the assassin and was gladdened to see him fall back as had his fellows. I then turned to see to the Count. Holmes was on the floor, struggling with the last man, whom he had somehow managed to disarm in the dim light, but they were now fighting for the possession of Holmes's firearm. I turned away from the Count and, seizing my revolver by its barrel, brought the heavy handle down on the would-be assassin's head, knocking him instantly unconscious.

Holmes scrambled to his feet.

"Once more, Watson, I owe you my life."

Holmes's praise was always welcome to me, but at that moment I had more important considerations on my mind.

As he grimaced in pain, I removed the Count's jacket and ripped open his shirt to examine the wound he had sustained. It was serious, but not fatal. The bullet had come out through his upper back, so there was much blood, but less danger of infection. I went down to the kitchen and boiled a kettle of water. In the bathroom I found an old but clean sheet which I ripped into strips. Entering the room once more, I cleaned the wound and bandaged it as best I could.

"You're wasting your time, Doctor, " the Count croaked. "In the end, they got what they wanted. I am dying."

"Nonsense", I retorted. "You'll be in the hospital for some time, true, but there's no reason why you shouldn't recover. You'll have a nasty pair of scars – but that's better than the alternative. I'll send Holmes for an ambulance."

I looked around. The man whose head I had cracked was nowhere to be seen – and where was my fellow lodger?

I later learned that while I had been preparing my makeshift bandages, Holmes had dragged his unconscious assailant down to the ground floor and bound his arms and legs with the sashes of the broken window. He then went into the street and ascertained that all three of the assassins who had climbed to the window were dead, two killed by gunshot and the other by a broken neck, sustained in his fall. The other two men who had come in by the door were likewise gone to meet their maker.

The gunshots had finally aroused the attention of the local constable on his beat, who blew his whistle to summon his nearest colleagues. They were, Holmes told me, at first reluctant to believe that this shabbily-dressed figure could be the renowned detective, but then a policeman with whom he had previously worked arrived on the scene and confirmed his identity. The surviving member of the Long Arm was bundled onto a police cart, and an ambulance summoned.

I have said before that often, when he had come to the conclusion of a demanding case, Holmes might be limp and listless, perhaps staying in his bed for several days. I must say that after the case of the Long Arm I had a somewhat similar reaction. I hadn't seen so much action in many years, nor did I take it lightly that I was responsible for the deaths of three men, however much they may have deserved to die. So it wasn't until some days later that I was ready to discuss it with Holmes.

I need not end this chronicle on such a sad note, for there was at least something of a happy ending. I never learned what became of Hannah Goldman, but Count Ridolfi made a full recovery and returned at last to his native land. Holmes's brother Mycroft had a word in the ear of a certain Gracious Lady, who communicated with her fellow-monarch, King Umberto I of Italy, to suggest that in consideration of his sterling work as Governor of Frascillata, Count Ridolfi should be given a pension and a suite of rooms in the palace, where the Royal Guard would keep him safe from any more attempts on his life.

The Adventure of the Rainsford Inheritance

During my long acquaintance with the world's first consulting detective, Mr. Sherlock Holmes, we encountered a wide variety of both clients and criminals. Sometimes Holmes was able to anticipate and prevent the commission of a crime, while in other instances it fell to us to ensure that the perpetrators of such misdeeds did not escape the consequences of their actions. We saw human nature at its worst, and at its best. The results of our efforts might be the prevention of an international catastrophe, or merely the survival or happiness of one or two individuals. Some cases – most of which, I confess, I have refrained from laying before the general public – revolved around murders of a particularly gruesome kind, but at the other end of the spectrum there were cases which, though they presented Holmes with an opportunity to exercise his powers, provided us with a welcome respite from the darker kind.

One such exploit was the matter of the Rainsford Inheritance, and while the happiness of a young woman depended upon its successful solution, I am sure my readers will concur that it is, in essence, a light-hearted tale.

It was a fine spring afternoon in early May. The sun was

pouring through the windows of our sitting room, and we had just finished one of Mrs. Hudson's fine lunches. I sat back in my usual chair and smoked a post-prandial cigar. Holmes had concluded a difficult and important case, the affair of the Balkan Miniatures, only the day before, and I had expected to see little or nothing of him until the following day, for on many such occasions he took to his bed in a state of nervous and physical exhaustion and remained there for long hours. It seemed, however, that the freshness and beauty of the morning had had the effect of invigorating him, for he joined me at breakfast in a cheery mood, then spent some time on a chemical experiment which, so far as I knew, had no connection with any criminal investigation he might be conducting. He then turned to answering some correspondence, which couldn't have been urgent as he waited until Mrs. Hudson brought up our midday meal before he handed the replies over to her to post. Knowing his mercurial nature, I had no idea how long this congeniality would last, or how long it would be before he demanded an intellectual challenge to prevent him from sliding into the slough of despondency.

Fortunately for my nerves, the question did not arise. About an hour after lunch, our doorbell rang, and shortly thereafter Mrs. Hudson showed a young woman of about twenty-two into our quarters. I stood up when the lady entered the room, and though I am only average height, the top of her head barely came up to the level of my shoulders. This, combined with her pale face, delicate features, and light blue eyes, and the neatness and simplicity of her attire, an ensemble of light green satin, gave the impression of a figurine of Dresden china come to life.

"Good afternoon, gentlemen," she said. "Which of you is Mr. Holmes?"

"I am Sherlock Holmes, and this – "

"Must be Dr. Watson."

"Your servant, Madam."

"Pray take a seat," said Holmes. "And you are?"

"My name is Anna Wheatley," she replied. "I hope that you will not find my problem too obvious or trivial to be of interest. I can, of course, recompense you for your time and trouble."

"That is something we may discuss later, though I perceive that money is in some manner at the heart of the question you intend to put in our hands."

Miss Wheatley lowered her eyes and a blush suffused her face.

"You are correct," she said, "though I cannot see how you could know it."

"Your outfit was fashionable two years ago, but it has gone out of style since then. The seam of the right sleeve has been resewn at least twice, probably by yourself, since the mends are visible. Moreover, the dress shows signs of having been taken in. Since your form is slim, I can only assume that this weight loss is attributable to a long-standing worry. And your hands," Holmes concluded, reaching over and gently turning one of them, "show signs that you have been doing work to which they aren't accustomed."

It being spring, Miss Wheatley wasn't wearing gloves, and I

saw that her palms were red, and that in places the top layer of skin had been rubbed away.

"It's true," she said. "I had hoped that I could present you with this problem without revealing the reason why I need the matter solved so urgently, but I see that nothing can be hidden from you. Very well, I shall give you the whole story."

"That would be the best course of action," I interjected soothingly.

"Since my mother died some years ago, my father, John Wheatley, has spiraled deeper and deeper into despair. His business – he inherited a bicycle factory from my grandfather – was making less and less with the decreasing amount of attention he paid to it, until I finally convinced him to sell it while there were still buyers who would give him a reasonable price. When the money from the sale came into his hands, he didn't invest it sensibly, as I suggested, but tried to increase it by gambling, for which he has no aptitude. He then turned to drink. Eventually I was forced to give the servants notice and take on the entire responsibility for the maintenance of the household. Now there has come a ray of hope, a light at the end of the tunnel, but a curious condition is attached to it."

"Ah," said Holmes.

"I had an uncle named Alistair Rainsford, my mother's older brother, Rainsford being her maiden name. I was very fond of him, and spent a lot of time with him as a child. I hadn't seen him for some years, as there seems to have been some quarrel between him and my father at some point. Uncle Alistair made some very successful investments and became a wealthy man, but my father would never have gone to him for help. Uncle Alistair was, to say the least, somewhat eccentric."

"You speak of him in the past tense," said Holmes. "I take it he has passed away."

"Yes, a couple of weeks ago. Shortly after he died, I received a letter from his lawyers informing me that as his only living relative, I was the sole beneficiary of his will, but there was a strange condition attached to it. He had hidden the will somewhere in his house – not even his lawyers know where – and that, in order to benefit from it, I had to find it. I'm not allowed to go in there and search thoroughly everywhere in the hope that I might discover it. No, I must work out exactly where it is, and then be able to go straight there and retrieve it. Accompanying the letter was a sheet of paper which is meant to help me find it – but of course, Uncle Alastair put it in code. I recall from my childhood that he was very fond of such tricks."

She reached into her reticule and pulled out a page covered with typed numbers and spaces.

"You said you were very fond of your uncle. Was the feeling mutual?"

"Oh, certainly. I spent a lot of time with him when my father was away on business. Why do you ask?"

"It means that he wanted you to find the answer. It isn't insoluble. He isn't torturing you. Rather, he is playing a game with you from beyond the grave." Miss Wheatley gave a rueful little smile.

"He loved playing all sorts of games during his lifetime, Mr. Holmes. In fact, he tried to teach me a little about codes, but I wasn't old enough to understand any but the most simple."

"Was your uncle married?"

"No, he was a lifelong bachelor."

"Did he have any romantic attachments of any kind?"

"I believe he was engaged to a girl called Claire as a young man, but she died of pneumonia before they could marry. I expect that's why he remained single. I'm afraid I can't recall her surname."

"Did he have a dog or a cat?"

"He had a dog at one stage."

"Its name?"

"Piper, I believe."

"One last question: Was any time limit placed on the solution? Must you find the will before a particular date?"

"No, Mr. Holmes, but you can surely tell from my story that I should like to have the answer as soon as possible, to save my father and myself from ruin."

"Of course. I have many calls on my time, but I assure you that I shall spend my every free moment on the solution. If you care to leave your card, I will send you a telegram when I have found it."

"Thank you, Mr. Holmes. I place my future in your hands."

"Well, Watson," said Holmes when Mrs. Hudson had closed the front door behind our visitor, "while I have no doubt that that young woman's plight has touched that chivalrous heart of yours,

I fear that you can be of little help. A case for pure cerebration."

"I should still like to know how you arrived at the solution, when you do."

"Of course, old friend. Now, it is still early, and there may yet be another client to call on us with a more urgent case, but unless and until that happens, I shall concentrate on Miss Wheatley's problem."

I went over to that small section of our shelves that contained my books and selected a collection of the short stories of Guy de Maupassant. Then I poured myself a whisky, lit another cigar, and settled into my chair to read while Holmes worked on the code. I looked across at him twice where he sat at his desk: First when he lit a match and ran the flame under the page, and then when he took out several sheets of paper and began to cut them up along some folds he had made in them. Otherwise, I remained wholly absorbed in the French writer's celebrated *Boule de Suif.*

No other client arrived to distract Holmes from his labours, and it was about an hour before our evening meal was due that the detective leaned back in his chair and gave a sigh of pleasure.

I looked up from my book.

"You have the solution, then."

"Yes, I have the solution."

"Well, what is it?"

"Patience, old friend, patience. You did say, did you not, that you wished to know how I arrived at it? I have been careful to keep a record of every step of the process. Let us see how long it takes you to come to the same conclusion. Here is the page with the code. Does anything strike you about the numbers?"

I took the paper from him and looked at it for a few moments.

24	14	25		11	9	11			5	20	
20	9	5		18	5	19			9	8	
24	8	19		5	1		8		9	23	
14	9	7	19	23	18		20	11			
9	9		19	9		5	20			2	14
14	6	14		4	5	7			5	9	
15	1		15	25	14	25	1	2			
5	8	22		15	20	1			20	16	

"The highest number here is twenty-five."

"What does that suggest to you?"

I thought for a second.

"The alphabet!"

"The alphabet. It was in any case hard to see what else it could be if any message was to be conveyed. So I replaced the numbers with letters, being careful to retain the original spacing, and this was the result."

He picked up another sheet of paper.

"One second, Holmes. Before we leave the original page – why did you run the flame of a match underneath it?"

"I was trying to ascertain the meaning of the irregular spacing, and it struck me that there might be invisible writing in the spaces."

"Invisible writing?"

"Yes. Lemon juice is the most commonly used, though there

are other liquids that will serve the same turn. If you apply heat to it, it turns brown and can be easily read. But there was no invisible writing in the spaces."

I took the second sheet from him.

X	N	Y		L	I	L		E	T	
T	I	E		R	E	S		I	H	
X	H	S		E	A		H	I	W	
N	I	G	S	W	R		T	L		
I	I		S	I		E	T		B	N
N	F	N		D	E	G		E	I	
O	A		O	Y	N	Y	A	B		
E	H	V		E	T	A		T	P	

Recalling the tragic affair of the Dancing Men, I began to count the number of times each letter occurred in the hope of determining which stood for *E*, *T*, and *A*, but Holmes divined what I was at and shook his head.

"This is too short an example – only sixty-four letters – for us to be sure of any letters other than *E*, and if you continue to count, you will see that *E* is itself the most frequently occurring letter, which tells against the idea that it is a simple substitution code of the kind Abe Slaney used to persecute the unfortunate Mrs. Cubitt."

"Why did you ask Miss Wheatley about Rainsford's fiancée? And his dog?"

"Because I thought at first that what we might have here was encoded by the use of what is sometimes called a *keyword*, and sometimes a *headword*. It is quite common when using this method for the compiler to use a familiar name or word as the keyword. If the word used was picked at random, or had a significance unknown to Miss Wheatley, then decipherment would be impossible. For reasons I shall demonstrate, the key word cannot contain any repeated letters. *Claire* does not, but given her tragic loss to illness, I thought it unlikely that Rainsford would use it in a frivolous manner. So I asked about the dog, but of course, the name *Piper* contains the letter *P* twice. Now, I anticipated that you would ask this question, so I have prepared an example. You will recall that, during the last round of Fenian attacks on the capital, Scotland Yard asked for my assistance in decoding some secret messages that passed between the conspirators. At one point, the Yard had a coded letter they found in the house of one suspect, and a short message which merely read, *Brighton-on-Sea*."

"But no one ever calls it that," I objected.

"No indeed, and for that reason, and the fact that the seaside town was never the target of an attack, I was led to the conclusion that it was the key to the decipherment of the letter. *Brighton-on-Sea*, the word, was really *Brighton on C*, the letter, and so I was able to compile this."

He handed me another paper, on which was written:

B R I G H T O N A C D E F J K L M P Q S U V W X Y Z
C D E F G H I J K L M N O P Q R S T U V W X Y Z A B

"And of the basis of this, you were able to prevent further atrocities and send an entire chapter of the organization to prison or the gallows."

"Just so. However, as I said, I came to the conclusion that it was not a substitution code of any kind. I wrestled with the significance of the spacing, and while I am one-hundred-percent sure that I have deciphered the message correctly, I confess that I am still unsure why it is laid out in that manner. In any event, after toying briefly with several other methods, I sat back and took a few moments to see if I could think of another way of tackling the problem. I hit on the possibility that rather than being encoded, the entire message was an anagram. A complex one, granted, but I was convinced that it was soluble by the application of logic, and so it proved to be. You saw me fold several pieces of paper and cut them into smaller pieces. One, in fact, for each of the sixty-four letters on the page. When I had finished the laborious task of writing a letter on each of the pieces, I considered the rest of the information the young lady had given us.

"If the will were hidden somewhere in the house, then the obvious thing to do was to see if the names of individual rooms were obtainable from the letters. Fortunately, the letters did not contain the word *room* itself, which enabled me to discard *bedroom, bathroom, dining room, living room, box room, spare room*, and so on. Three words which were obtainable were *hall, pantry*, and *library*. Of these three, I considered that the library was the most likely and decided to proceed on that supposition.

So I took out the letters for *library*. I considered it likely that the message also contained the words, *the will* so I discarded the letters of those words as well, This left me with:

*XNYITIEESIHXSEHNIGSWTISIETNNF
NDEGEIOAOYNABEHVETATP*

"I mentally reviewed a list of words appertaining to the contents of libraries. I could not get the word *book*, as there was no *K*, but the word *page* was there, so perhaps the will was stuck to a particular page in a particular book. If that were so, the name of the book would be there too, but obviously, that would come near the end, because at this point it would be impossible to deduce it. I removed the word *page*, so what remained was:

*XNYITIEESIHXSHNISWTISIETNNFND
EGEIOAOYNABEHVETT*

"I been worried about those *X*'s, but now I realized that if I had *page*, then it had to have a number, which might be six, sixteen or sixty, or sixty-something. Sixty-six would use both *X*'s. Then it occurred to me that if someone respected books enough to have a library, they were unlikely to paste anything to the page of a book, because its removal could damage the book. But they might put it between two pages, and I had the word *between*, so I took it out.

X N Y I T I S I H X S H N I S T I S I E T N F N D E G E I
O A O Y N A H V E T

"Now I needed two consecutive numbers. I could get *five* and *six*, *six* and *seven*, *seven* and *eight*, *eight* and *nine*, and *nine* and *ten*, but I thought the other *X* was probably part of a number, too. I had two *Y*'s, so I took *sixty* out twice. Then I realised that I needed *pages*, instead of *page*. I had to take another *S* out.

"I could make *sixty-seven* and *sixty-eight*, or *sixty-eight* and *sixty-nine*, but I had no basis upon to decide which, so I went back and looked over what I had already done. Assuming Rainsford had made a grammatical sentence, which as a literate person I imagined he had, I would need a *the* before the word *library*, and *and* between the two numbers, whatever they were. Out they came.

N I H N I I S I N F N E G E I O A O H V E T

"That was of no immediate help, because I could still make *seven*, *eight*, and *nine*. Then I thought, there is a strong possibility that we need the word *is*. *The will is*. I couldn't do anything like *the will can be found*, or *the will has been hidden*. If I used *is*, then the number couldn't contain *seven*, because there was only one *S* left. I took out *is*, *eight*, and *nine*. And of course, you will understand, that for the will to be between them, the first number must be even and the second odd. That left:

N I H I F N O A O V E

"I was beginning to have my suspicions about the name of the book, and when I took it out I was left with *of* and *in* which confirmed that my deduction was correct. Perhaps you would care to see if you can work it out for yourself."

And he handed me another paper on which was written:

H I N A O V E

"All one word?"

"All one word."

I gazed at it, prepared to be baffled as I so often was by Holmes's feats of intellect, but then I suddenly saw what it must be, and said, with a laugh of triumph, "*Ivanhoe!*"

"Yes, Watson – *Ivanhoe*. Now I had all the pieces before me, and all that remained was to arrange them into a coherent sentence."

And he passed me one final piece of paper, on which I read:

THE WILL IS IN THE LIBRARY BETWEEN PAGES SIXTY-EIGHT AND SIXTY-NINE OF IVANHOE

"Bravo!" I cried.

"Thank you, Watson. And now it only remains to inform Miss Wheatley of her good fortune. But that, I fear, must wait until the morning – " He glanced over at the clock upon the mantelpiece. " – as it is too late to send a telegram now. Pray ring for Mrs. Hudson, and see if dinner is ready, as I find I suddenly have quite an appetite."

After we had finished our dinner – veal and ham pie with haricot beans and glazed carrots, followed by apple pie and custard, all washed down with a fine claret – I picked up the second piece of paper to see if I could find any reason for the inclusion of the odd spaces which had defeated even Holmes. On a whim I took a pencil and drew the following diagram in my notebook, eliminating the spaces altogether:

X	N	Y	L	I	L	E	T
T	I	E	R	E	S	I	H
X	H	S	E	A	H	I	W
N	I	G	S	W	R	T	L
I	I	S	I	E	T	B	N
N	F	N	D	E	G	E	I
O	A	O	Y	N	Y	A	B
E	H	V	E	T	A	T	P

After a few minutes contemplation, I cried, "Holmes! Holmes!"

The detective looked up from the book he had been reading. "Yes?"

"I have discovered the reason for the spaces!"

"And what might that be?"

"They were there as a distraction, to divert any would-be solver from the fact that that without them, the message is a square of eight by eight."

I stood and handed him the notebook.

"Look at the *T* in the top right-corner, then, go down to *H* and read each diagonal line from right to left."

"*The will is in the* – Why, Watson, I should have handed you the paper straight away and saved myself an afternoon's labour!"

For all that Holmes had occasional bouts of vanity, he was, to do him justice, capable of taking a joke at himself, and he laughed in his quiet fashion for a minute or two.

"Well, well, I must console myself with the fact that no intellectual effort is ever truly wasted," he said, "and besides, it provided me with a few hours harmless entertainment. Bravo!"

Miss Wheatley returned the following day in response to Holmes's telegram, looking just as fragile and delicate as she had on her previous visit. When he handed her the paper, she fell into a chair and began to laugh so long and hard that Holmes and I exchanged glances. But before I could go over to my medical valise to obtain a sedative, her laughter subsided.

"Forgive me, gentlemen. It is just that my dear old uncle has played a last little joke upon me. He was a great admirer of Sir Walter Scott. The novels, the poems, the short stories, everything. He was always trying to encourage me to read him, so in the end I tried reading *Ivanhoe* and I absolutely hated it! Now he has made it crucial to my happiness. Mr. Holmes, Dr. Watson, I cannot thank you enough. My family's fortunes will be restored and I shall be able to concentrate on caring for my father. Rest assured that when I have full control of Uncle Alistair's estate, you will not find me ungenerous. But you can understand that I wish to be at my uncle's house as soon as possible, so please forgive me if I cut this interview short."

"Of course," "I replied. "We are most proud to have done you this service. "

The lady hurried down into Baker Street and hailed a cab.

Some weeks later, Holmes received, along with a letter of further thanks, a cheque from Miss Wheatley for the princely sum of £350.

"A young woman who is true to her word", Holmes remarked. "Now, Watson, Jacometti is appearing in *Cavalleria Rusticana* at Covent Garden this evening, and we can afford a box. There is time for a meal at L'Escargot d'Argent before the curtain goes up."

"Splendid," I said, and reached for my coat.

The Most Terrible Murderer

October 1903

My dear Watson,

*Can you extricate yourself from the toils of domestic
bliss long enough to join me for dinner at Baker Street
on this coming Thursday evening at half-past seven?*

Holmes

"Who is it from, John?"

I looked up from the brief note and across the breakfast table
at my wife of eleven months. At times I still found it difficult to
believe that this charming and sensitive woman had become a
permanent fixture in my life, and was bound to me in holy
matrimony.

"It's from Holmes, my dear. I'm invited to dinner on
Thursday."

Emily put her coffee cup down into the saucer and smiled.

"Then you must go, John. You haven't seen each other for
such a while."

It was true. Since the former Emily Manning had accepted
my hand in marriage, and I had resumed my medical practice, this
time in Queen Anne Street, the demands of work and domesticity

had drastically reduced the amount of time I had to spare for my old friend and former fellow-lodger. I still retained my notes from the many investigations on which I had accompanied him, and had even given over some of my brief leisure time to casting one or two of them into narrative form. The last time I had been in contact with him had been to ask his permission to someday publish a story which we had previously decided should be suppressed for an indeterminate period.

"Well, I shall, then, if you don't object."

Emily took my hand and kissed it.

"Ah, my devoted husband! I think I can survive an evening without you, and you and he are such old friends, how could I object?"

Even as the cab turned into Baker Street that autumn evening, my mind was flooded with memories. Our first meeting in the laboratory at Barts. The sudden appearance of the giant rat of Sumatra. The awful revelation of the true identity of the Whitechapel killer. The crude stick figures of the dancing men. Merridew, who slit his own throat before our eyes, rather than face trial and an inevitable journey to the gallows. The odious Charles Augustus Milverton and his well-deserved end. And so much else – including, of course, Mary. It is a lucky man who knows such a love but once, and I have known it more often.

So familiar was the door of 221b Baker Street that I almost reached into my pocket for my key, but I caught myself, left the key where it was, and rang the bell.

The door was opened by a familiar figure.

"Mrs. Hudson! How are you?"

"Oh, I'm well enough," replied the housekeeper. "And I can see Mrs. Watson has been taking good care of you!"

"She has indeed. And Holmes?"

"Oh, you know him. The only time he's ever ill is when he's run himself into the ground over some case he's been investigating. He'll be pleased to see you. He has a little surprise for you."

"A surprise?"

"Yes."

She took my hat and coat.

"Go straight up. Dinner will be served in five minutes."

I climbed the steps to our old rooms. As I opened the door, I saw Holmes sitting in his accustomed chair, still his old self, clad in his disreputable dressing gown, his clay pipe clenched between his teeth and his hands steepled in front of him. He was not alone, however. A prosperous-looking man in his mid-forties, with a head of curly brown hair and a full beard speckled with grey, was seated in my old armchair. My first thought was that the man was a client, and about to leave, but he sprang from the chair and seized me by the hand.

"Dr. Watson! It's wonderful to see you once more!"

"Good Heavens!" I cried, in sudden recognition. "It's Murray!"

"How long has it been, Doctor? Twenty-two years? Twenty-three?"

"Since you came to see me in the base hospital in Peshawar. Holmes, you know this man saved my life?"

"I had heard something of the kind."

It was Murray who, after I had been wounded by a Jezail bullet at the Battle of Maiwand, had thrown me across a pack-horse and got me back to the British lines, at no small danger to himself.

"This is indeed a pleasant surprise, "I said. What have you been doing with yourself, old chap? You look as if you've come a good way in this world."

"After I left the army, I stayed in India and got a position managing a tea plantation in Assam. Well, I made a good job of it, if I do say so myself, and pretty soon I was managing a larger one, and made some sound investments with the money I earned."

"What brings you back to England?"

"My wife passed away – "

"My dear fellow, I'm sorry to hear it!"

" – and so I thought I'd come back to the old country. I could have obtained your address from your publisher, but I confess I was eager to meet Mr. Holmes as well as to see you again, so I came to Baker Street, and he was kind enough to arrange this meeting."

At this point, Mrs. Hudson brought up the first course of what proved to be an excellent dinner. Holmes said little while we ate, but smiled once or twice as Murray and I recalled our far-off days in the Jewel in the Crown of the Empire. When the meal was over, however, and we were smoking and taking a glass of brandy,

Murray looked over to Holmes and said, "I'd like to ask you something, if I may."

Holmes drew on his cigar and said, "Please do, Mr. Murray."

"Well. I've read all of Dr. Watson's accounts of your cases, and enjoyed them all."

Here he turned to me and said, "I must say, I gained a little fame amongst the expatriate community by being the man who indirectly made your stories possible. But you often mention cases that remain untold. I'm not asking you to break any confidences, of course, but I am curious about them. For example, Mr. Holmes, who would you say was the worst murderer you ever had to deal with?"

"That very much depends on how you are defining 'worst'," said Holmes. "Dr. Grimesby Roylott only did away with one person, but his method of doing so was diabolical. Baron Adelbert Gruner more than once made an unsuspecting woman fall in love with him before it served his turn to kill her. Alfred Tarleton tortured his victims for some time before finally dispatching them, while Dr. Henry Staunton made a habit of killing his elderly patients after ensuring that they had remembered him in their will."

"Then there was Schofield, who murdered the whole Abernetty family," I said, "and Vigor, the so-called 'Hammersmith Wonder', a circus performer who used his powers of contortion to break into people's houses and rob and kill them in their sleep."

I was about to add the notorious Jack the Ripper, but I recalled just in time that we had agreed never to mention our connection to the case, let alone the true identity of the killer.

"And yet, Watson, I think you will agree that the most, shall we say, unsettling murderer we have ever encountered was Bert Stevens."

"Yes, indeed."

"What was it about him that set him apart?" asked Murray.

"It is an axiom of our profession, Mr. Murray, that one should not permit one's judgment to be biased by personal qualities. To do so is to depart from the road of clear reason, which is the only true path to the facts. Elspeth Carson, to give but one example, was a charming young woman, beloved by all who knew her, but she ended on the gallows for murdering three small children.

"Bert Stevens was perhaps the most extreme case of this dichotomy between appearance and reality that I have ever encountered. He was mild-mannered, soft-spoken and gentle in his ways. But beneath that placid surface lay a fiendish, calculating intelligence, untroubled by conscience. But if you would wish to hear the whole story – "

"Yes, I certainly would,"

" – then I hand you over to Watson. He, as you know, is the storyteller." He stood and went over to the bookcase.

"You may need this," he said, taking his casebook for the relevant year from its shelf. He opened it to the date in question, handed it to me, then returned to his seat.

"Thank you, Holmes."

"I shall only interject when I deem it necessary."

I took a moment to light a fresh cigar and gather my thoughts, then I began . . . .

The Events of June 1887

"Inspector Merivale, one of the better Scotland Yard men, and a friend to us both, called on us one evening in late June to discuss a rash of seemingly unconnected killings which had recently taken place in the metropolis. Now, it was unusual to have so many murders committed in such a short space of time – "

"Well," said Holmes, "that statement needs a little modification. It's unusual to have so many *unsolved* murders in such a short span of time. In most cases, it's obvious who the perpetrator is. A man kills his wife in a fit of jealous rage, another bludgeons his mate to death in an outburst of drunken anger – these stories are on the back pages of the newspapers, if they make it into the news at all. They'll be on the front page if the victims or the murderers are known to polite society, but otherwise – Well, there are murders being committed every day, but most of the public are unaware of the majority of them."

"Merivale asked if it were possible that they were all being committed by the same man, and Holmes replied that it was unlikely."

"Indeed," said Holmes. "It is actually quite rare for someone to kill more than one person, and when they do, the victims, if not known to the murderer, are at least usually members of the same profession or social class, and usually killed in the same way. The Polish murderer, Marek Wesolowski, or Thomas Kelly as he was known when he lived in London, killed four of his mistresses by the gradual administration of poison. Then there's the Whitechapel Killer, of course. He did away with at least five East End prostitutes. Perhaps he knew them, perhaps he didn't. He probably strangled them, then cut their throats and disembowelled them. He did more than that to his last victim, but then he killed her in her room, not out on the street."

"So," I continued, "we went through the victims with Merivale, one by one, as we shall now.

"First, Pierre Blanchard, twenty-four, a shopkeeper and a native of Dijon, found strangled in Eldon Street, Stepney, 11:30 p.m. He'd been dead for about two hours. From the marks on the neck, the strangulation appeared to have been carried out by the use of a broad ligature – a cummerbund, perhaps, or a scarf."

"Next was Robert Carver, draper, thirty-four, his wife Sophie, twenty-six, and draper's assistant Martin Ball, seventeen. They were all found in Carver's rooms above his shop in Putney at 7:30 a.m., 15th April. Their heads had been beaten to a pulp by some heavy instrument. They had all been dead between four-and-a-half and five hours. Then, let me see – yes, Jean Dawson, aged only sixteen, found in a dustbin behind Artillery Buildings,

Victoria Street, 24th April, at six a.m. Her throat had been slit, her body was naked and completely drained of blood – "

"Oh, God!"

"Are you all right, Murray? Do you want to stop?"

"No, no, I'm fine, it's just – sixteen, for God's sake! And in a damned dustbin! What kind of monster could do such a thing?"

"Merivale suggested a vampire, and I of course said that there were no such things, but he pointed out that there had been killers who drank their victims' blood. Human vampires, you might say. What was the name of that man in Harrogate, in '84?"

"Walter Harvey," said Holmes, "and yes, he did drink some of his victims' blood after he'd killed them, but this would still be a problem: Jean Dawson must have been quite small if she could be stuffed in a dustbin, but even so, she must have had six or seven pints of blood in her body. The police medical examiner determined she'd been dead between two and three hours. The body was completely drained. The killer could have drunk six pints of water in that time, or even six pints of beer, but six pints of blood? He would feel ill after a pint, even if he were really determined to carry it through. No, I came to the conclusions that the body must have been hung upside down and drained somewhere else, then dumped where it was found."

I turned to the following page in the casebook.

"The next was Constable Ernest Romney, thirty-one. He was found in the Edgware Road at 10:25 p.m., May 2nd. He had a bullet wound to the chest, and he'd been dead between one and two hours. Only one of the other victims was shot, and that was in the head."

"Sad to say," observed Holmes, "policemen get killed on duty quite often, so while it certainly counts as an unsolved murder, it might have been even less likely to be connected to any of the others."

"Next we had Mehmed Kartal, secretary to the Turkish ambassador, twenty-seven. He was found in his rooms in Bayswater Road, at seven a.m. on the 15th May. He'd been dead five to six hours, and killed in a most bizarre fashion: A metal spike had been driven through his skull and into his brain."

"It does sound like an odd thing to kill someone with," said Murray.

"It does indeed," said Holmes. "Most murders are unpremeditated, with the killer using the first weapon that comes to hand. Even when a murder is planned, there is still a fairly narrow range of methods employed – poison, strangulation, a gun, a knife, or a blunt object."

"It was at this point, as I recall, Holmes, that you were beginning to suspect that there might, after all, be a connection between these killings, and there was but one perpetrator rather than several."

"Correct. I had, of course, been keeping a weather eye on the progress of the investigations, but it wasn't until we actually sat down with Merivale and began to discuss them together that that connection started to become clear. Now, Mr. Murray, I must tell you that in those little sketches of his, my good friend Watson here habitually exaggerates my abilities. While I own that I have brought the arts of observation and deduction, and of reasoning from cause to effect, to greater heights than any man living, I am still human, and so fall short of perfection. This is particularly true when one considers the fact that I have made it my business to study the crimes of the past, in order to see what light they may throw on the misdeeds of the present.

"The killer, whoever he was, was recreating some of those crimes of bygone days. Let us again take them one by one.

"Pierre Blanchard had been strangled using a ligature. Now, as someone who, like Watson, has served on the Indian sub-continent, you may have heard of the *Thugs*, or the *Phansigars*, as they are sometimes called."

"Yes, indeed."

"The British administration broke the cult in the 1830's. Their most prolific assassin was a man called Behram, who claimed to have had over nine-hundred victims. They worshipped Kali the Destroyer, and the story is that once Kali was fighting a demon, and every time she cut him with her sword, another demon sprang from each drop of blood that the demon shed, until she was fighting an army of them. She defeated them by strangling them, so that no more blood would fall. So her worshippers killed in the same way, using strips of cloth called *rumals*. They mainly killed travellers, and looked on their victims as sacrifices to appease the goddess, who would otherwise destroy the whole human race.

"Robert Carver and his wife, and Carver's unfortunate assistant, were killed in emulation of what are known as the Ratcliff Highway murders, in 1811. There were seven in all, the weapon in each case being a maul, a type of sledgehammer. The probable killer was a sailor called John Williams, who was staying near the Highway at a house in Wapping. He committed suicide before he could be put on trial.

"Now, Mr. Murray, have you heard of Countess Elizabeth Bathory?"

"The name is vaguely familiar."

"She is perhaps better known by her sobriquet, '*The Blood Countess*'. She was a sixteenth-century Hungarian noblewoman who became obsessed with the idea that bathing in the blood of young girls would restore her youth and beauty. She drained hundreds of teenaged girls of their blood over the course of two or three years. The highest estimate is over nine-hundred."

"Surely it would have obvious fairly soon that it wasn't working," said Murray.

"I'm sure you're right," said Holmes, "but it may have been a case of '*The Emperor's New Clothes*'. None of her servants had the courage to tell her that her youth and beauty were not returning, so the killings continued. It must be clear that it was her history which inspired the death of young Jean Dawson."

"What happened to this Bathory woman?"

"She was tried and sentenced to spend the rest of her life in one tiny room with no windows and only a small aperture to pass food and drink through to her. She died after a couple of years.

"The murder of Constable Romney was more difficult to place, because, as I said, policeman are killed with greater frequency than the bulk of the population. But working on the basis that our putative killer was modelling his crimes on those of well-known murderers, I surmised that in this instance he was following in the footsteps of Charles Peace, whose first victim was Constable Nicholas Cock of the Manchester Constabulary, in 1876."

"Which brings us to the case of Mehmed Kartal and the iron spike," I said.

"Yes," said Holmes, "and to explain that we must once again look back through time. In fifteenth-century Wallachia, now part of Romania, there was a *voivode*, or warlord, called Vlad Dracula."

"I've read that book," said Murray." Are we back with vampires?"

"I've met Bram Stoker – " I said.

"Yet another purveyor of fantastical tales."

"Thank you, Holmes. I was about to say, Stoker used the name, but his story has little or no connection to the historical character."

"Dracula was also known as *Vlad Tepes*, which means *Vlad the Impaler*. It was his habit to punish people by pushing long wooden spikes through various parts of their anatomy and leaving them to die a lingering and extremely painful death. Now it was unlikely that our killer, whoever he was, would be carrying a long wooden spike around, by day or by night, but his method fitted another story that was told of Dracula, and perhaps explained the choice of Mehmed Kartal as a victim: Dracula spent most of his life in conflict with the Turks, and on one occasion he was visited by three emissaries from the Turkish sultan, Murad II. He asked them to remove their turbans, and when they refused to do so, he had them nailed to their heads with iron spikes."

"So," I said, "Holmes had established the principle on which the murders were being committed, but how were we to know where the killer would strike next?"

"It seemed odd to me," said Holmes, "that someone who was copying the crimes of previous murderers should choose such an eclectic mix, from a wide range of places and times. We've had enough homegrown killers here in Britain over the last fifty years to supply a variety of motives and methods. This suggested to me either that the culprit was, like myself, a student of the history of crime, or had some other formula for choosing to emulate those particular criminals in that particular sequence. If the former were true, then the order might be completely random, which would make a solution virtually impossible. Clearly, it was not chronological, either backwards or forwards. What little we do know of multiple murderers suggests that their behaviour follows a pattern. We had to find out what that pattern was, and where it came from. I think you can stop there, Watson. There were more victims, but it was at this stage of our investigation that I began to formulate a theory as to what that pattern might be."

"Yes," I recalled, "Merivale left us at about half-past ten, and Holmes asked him to call again the following afternoon."

"I must say," said Murray, "this is just like one of your stories, Watson. Better, because it's straight from the horse's mouth. It's pretty grim, though, isn't it?"

"That's one reason why any account of it will stay unpublished for many years after we are gone. After Merivale arrived the following day, we walked together along Baker Street and into Marylebone Road. We visited a particular establishment there that you may have heard of: Madame Tussaud's Waxworks."

"I think I begin to see," said Murray.

"We made our way to the front of the queue, amidst much complaint from the assembled customers, and gained immediate admittance when Merivale displayed his identification. Once we were inside, Holmes led us to a particular part of the museum."

"The Chamber of Horrors!"

"Correct, Mr. Murray," said Holmes.

"We walked past wax *tableaux* of inquisitors torturing heretics, Jacobins guillotining aristocrats, Viking archers riddling Edward the Martyr with arrows, and Romans about to immolate bound Christians during the reign of the Emperor Domitian, until we came to a separate room devoted to representations of individual murderers.

"There were twenty main figures: Marek Wesolowski, Behram the Thug, John Williams, Elizabeth Bathory, Charles Peace, Vlad the Impaler, and the ones I haven't mentioned: Christopher Mills, whose charming habit was to shoot random people through the head, and who was caught when one of his victims unexpectedly survived and identified him – Guiseppe Cardoni, an Italian garrotter whom the Turks employed during the Greek War of Independence, Lu Mei Hua, who killed several of her rivals for the affections of the warlord Zhang Chang by stabbing them through the heart with a long pin, and Michael Bennett, a waterman who cudgelled and robbed some of his passengers and then threw them into the Thames to drown. Each of them, too, had had murders modelled on their crimes, and the killer no doubt intended to emulate the other miscreants represented in this grim tableau.

"'My God!' said Merivale, as we went slowly round the room at Holmes's instigation, weaving through the other visitors and looking at each exhibit.

"'They're all here, in that exact order,' I said.

"'Except for one," said Merivale, pointing to his left. 'Behram isn't the first.' The figure of Marek Wesolowski, alias Thomas Kelly, was standing closest to the entrance on that side.

"'I believe I have an explanation for that,' said Holmes.

"'Apart from Kelly, the murderer acted in accordance with the order of the wax figures,' said Merivale.

"'Holmes! There are twenty figures in here! Will there be eleven more murders?'

"'No, Watson, nine. And we can prevent them from happening.'

"He turned decisively, and Merivale and I followed him back out to the foyer.

"'We should like to speak to the curator,' Holmes said to the young woman at the cash desk. Having seen Merivale's police card, she left her position, led us down a corridor, and into an area cordoned off by ropes which bore a sign on the wall bearing the message, *"No Entry to the Public"*. She indicated a door marked *"R. Pemberton, Curator"* and then left us to return to her position.

"'Best if you identify yourself first, Merivale,' said Holmes. 'The presence of an officer of the law tends to reassure those in a position of authority.'

"Pemberton recognised our names – "

"'Of course,' said Murray. 'Practically everyone has read your stories.'

"I glanced across at Holmes, who made a mock grimace.

"Pemberton was a middle-aged man of about my height," he said. "Very dapper, his moustache waxed and teased into a point at either end, and he had a silver *pince-nez* perched on the end of the bridge of his long nose.

"'So, gentlemen,' he said, 'how may I be of use to you?'

"'How many attendants do you have working for you?' asked Holmes.

"Pemberton went behind his large mahogany writing desk, opened a drawer, and pulled out a brown folder.

"'About thirty,' he said with a smile. 'I try to be methodical. I have to be. I don't have a terribly good memory. They're all in here: Names, ages, pay, shift patterns, prev – '

"'Shift patterns?'

"'Oh, yes. We have to have guards here at night. Would you believe it, people have actually been known to break in and try and steal things from the figures – Napoleon's hat, the arrow in King Harold's eye, Queen Victoria's veil. I don't know if they think they're the real things, but anyway, we had to put a stop to it.'

"'Have any of your attendants been widowed recently?'

"'Yes, one has. What's his name? I told you my memory was bad. Ah, wait a minute – Stevens. Bertram Stevens, that's it.'

"'Can I see his records?'

"'Certainly.'

Pemberton opened the folder and leafed through it until he found Stevens' sheet, then handed it to Holmes.

"'You're on a case,' said Pemberton as Holmes ran his eyes down the page.

"'Well deduced, Mr. Pemberton.'

"'I hope you don't suspect Stevens of anything. I've never met anyone less like a criminal. He's a devout churchgoer. Man wouldn't hurt a fly. Meek and mild. Very quiet – even more so since he lost his wife.'

"'May I take this?'

"'If you bring it back.'

"'Of course.'

"Once we were back in the open air, Holmes suggested that we repair to the nearby Carpenter's Arms.

"'So, Mr. Holmes,' said Merivale as the bartender brought three foaming pints over to our table, 'may we take it that Bertram Stevens is your suspect?'

"'That's correct. Merivale, you pointed out that Kelly was the first of the wax figures, not Behram.'

"The Scotland Yarder took a sip of his beer. "'Yes, and you said you could explain it, that it didn't spoil your theory.'

"'And it doesn't. For what was Kelly executed?'

"'He poisoned four of his common-law wives,' said Merivale.

"'Four of them?" I said. 'How many did he have?'

"'He had a legal wife in Poland, and at least six mistresses in London – all of whom called themselves "Mrs. Kelly" at some point.'

"'All four died of antimony poisoning,' said Holmes, 'given in the form of tartar emetic, a means of inducing vomiting. They all had the same symptoms, but Wesolowski – or Kelly if you prefer – wasn't arrested, or even suspected, until the fourth one died. So, if Stevens killed his wife by tartar emetic, given in gradual doses, the same as Kelly, he might not have been suspected either, particularly since he didn't kill anyone else in that fashion.'

"'Well,' said Merivale, 'we can get an exhumation order for Mrs. Stevens" body, and we can make enquiries at the chemist's in Stevens" immediate area to see if he bought tartar emetic in any of them. It's a poison, so there should be a record.'

"I had been drinking silently, but now I said, 'I can see a couple of problems, Holmes.'

"'Go on.'

"'Supposing Stevens had his wife cremated? And what if he didn't buy the poison in a chemist in his area? Are the police going to inquire at every chemist shop in London?'

"'Well, that's been done in the past, but I take your point. As for the cremation, that costs more than burial, and Stevens is not in a particularly well-paid job.'

"'Why did you take that sheet of Stevens' shift patterns?'

"'It may at least demonstrate that he was free to carry out the murders at the correct dates and times, though I concede that that is only corroborative if we have more evidence of his guilt.'

"A chemist in Bow Road testified that Stevens had purchased several packets of tartar emetic four months before his wife's death. On this basis, an exhumation order was granted on Mrs. Stevens' corpse in the Roman Catholic cemetery in Leytonstone, and it was found to contain a significant amount of antimony. Stevens was arrested and held in Pentonville Prison pending trial.

"Holmes and I were permitted to sit on the first interrogation carried out by Merivale at Scotland Yard, with a sergeant also in attendance. As soon as Stevens was brought into the room, I understood what Pemberton had said about the unlikelihood of his being a criminal.

"He was short, with wispy, wavy blond hair, a pale, pinched face, and behind wire-rimmed spectacles, large, china-blue eyes that seemed filled with a lasting sadness. His legs were slightly bowed, and I attributed this to rickets, which, along with the general frailty of his physique, suggested that he had suffered malnutrition as a child. Was it possible that this feeble creature had perpetrated such a string of atrocities?

"He sat down and looked from one to the other of us, with a seraphic smile.

"'Now, Stevens,' Merivale began, 'do you know why you are here?'

"'I am afraid I have no idea, but I put my trust in the Lord.'

"The sound of his voice was barely above a whisper, his demeanour modest and self-effacing.

"'Do you deny that you bought eight packets of tartar emetic at Boyson's in Bow Road four months before the death of your wife Sarah?'

"'Is that when it was? No, I don't deny it, if that's what the man at the chemist's says.'

"'Why did you purchase so much?'

"'Sarah had a tapeworm.'

"'But she didn't go to a doctor.'

"'She refused. Her mother died in hospital, which made her suspicious of the medical profession. I read that tartar emetic could be used against parasites, but I did not know how long it would take, so I bought a great deal of it. I talked to our vicar, and he advised me to pray, so I did, every night, but in the end it pleased God to take her.'

"'And that's how you explain the high levels of antimony in her body, is it?'

"Those blue eyes widened and tears welled up in them.

"'I – I don't like to say it, but I am rather afraid that she may have taken her own life. Please, please, don't say anything! I couldn't stand it if she were reburied in unconsecrated ground!'"

"Before Merivale could answer, Holmes interposed. 'You know, Stevens, there's one thing I don't understand.'

"'Wh – what's that?'

"'How someone as intelligent as you could make such a stupid mistake.'

"'I don't know what you mean.'

"'I imagine it was because you were just starting out. You were much more careful with the other killings. They were masterfully done.'

"A strange change gradually came over Stevens' face. The shy, childlike meekness began to recede. His expression held hints of both cunning and pride, but he repeated, though with less conviction, 'I don't know what you mean.'

"'I suppose killing Constable Romney must have been fairly easy, but I'm still trying to work out how you got Jean Dawson's body into that dustbin.'

"Stevens was now looking Holmes in the eye, as if to stare him down, but he said nothing.

"'And as for the iron spike in Kartal's skull – that was a stroke of genius. It took me some time to understand the reference.'

"Stevens' head pulled back until he was looking down his nose at my friend.

"'Do you know who I am?' said the detective. 'I'm Sherlock Holmes. You must have heard the name. And you baffled even me.'

"A self-satisfied smile spread across the murderer's face, which was now utterly transformed from a picture of uncomprehending innocence to one of arrogance, horribly tinged with a hint of glee at his crimes.

"'Even Sherlock Holmes,' he said. 'So, I shall have a special place in the annals of crime.'

"I shuddered. Twelve people had died at this man's hand, in a variety of grisly ways, and here he was, smiling.

"'Do you admit to these killings then, Stevens?' demanded Merivale.

"'My only regret is that I was unable to bring the work to a conclusion. Yes, yes, Mr. Whatever-your-name-is Policeman, I was the artist.'

"Once he had made his admission, Stevens waxed garrulous and began to go into the killings in detail. Holmes and I stood to leave.

"'As it says in *Proverbs*, "*Pride goeth before destruction, and an haughty spirit before a fall*,"'" Holmes remarked as we walked out into the open air . . . .

"That," said Murray, "was a remarkable tale."

"There's a little more," I said. "I see you kept the clipping from *The South London Sentinel*, Holmes. One of the radical newspapers," I explained to Murray. "Let me read it aloud:

The public has recently heard much about the shocking series of murders perpetrated by Bertram Stevens, and while it is not our business to condone these actions, we would argue that a little may be said in mitigation. We quote Sir Anthony Brocklebank, the noted alienist:

"Bertram Stevens was found abandoned on the steps of the Sacred Heart and cared for by the nuns until the age of seven, when he was placed in the workhouse at Hunslet in the West Riding of Yorkshire. There he was provided with education, and just about learned to read and write, but was generally deemed ineducable and incapable of adopting a trade. He did show the beginnings of an aptitude for music, but this was not encouraged, and there were no instruments available on which he might develop an ability.

"Around the age of twelve or thirteen he began to show signs of mental disturbance. He would go into trance states without warning, and when he recovered, earned the scorn of his fellow-inmates by claiming that he had visited far-distant and beautiful lands. He responded to their jibes with uncontrolled violence and invariably received a thorough beating in return. At other times he said that he was really the son of the King of France, or of Italy, and that very soon his father would send a coach for him to take him

away, and again, no beating would shake this conviction, whether it was given by his fellows or by the adults in charge. At the age of fifteen, he was sent from the workhouse, devoid of prospects, with no-one in the world who cared a jot about him. He made his way to London.

"Somehow, Stevens learned to suppress the problematic aspects of his personality and appear 'normal', I would imagine as a survival mechanism. Indeed, those who encountered him described him as meek, soft-spoken, and deeply religious. This assumption of 'normality' is doubtless what enabled him to find a wife and get his job at the wax museum. All this I have gathered from conversations with him and what I have inferred from his records. What I am about to say is speculative, though there is little doubt in my mind that it is the truth: What we have here is a man who has no clear identity. What slender chances he had to form the beginnings of a healthy personality, such as his musical ability, were taken from him or not allowed to develop. He escaped, into oblivion or into fantasy, but these earned him scorn and violence.

"By the time he began work at the museum, he was what we might term a 'Jekyll and Hyde', or multiplex personality, a divided consciousness fitting in with the norms and conventions of society on the surface, but in the deeper recesses of his psyche, full

176

of a repressed need to express anger and violence. Now, the way he explained it to me is that he was 'possessed' – that was the word he used – by the spirits of these murderers, that they took him over one by one and sent him forth to do the same 'work' they had done. I have no doubt that that is what he believed to be the truth. My own interpretation is that on those nights when he was left alone with the wax figures, having few or no inner resources to distract him from brooding upon them, he would read the descriptive passages in front of each figure, and began to admire them – perhaps, for their defiance of the law and conventional human conduct.

"And so, working his way round the room, having no true identity of his own, he took on one persona after another, killing once in each identity, but each time finding it unsatisfying, and moving on to the next in the hope that another murder would bring balm to his soul. What he would have done had he managed to inhabit all twenty and remained unsatisfied, I don't know. Suicide, perhaps."

"Thank you, Watson. I say now, as I said then, that while I can feel compassion for the child he was, I have nothing but contempt for the man he became. To carry out those murders required meticulous planning and cold intelligence, and I have no doubt that what Brocklebank encountered was yet another false persona, geared to appeal to what Stevens must have sensed the alienist wanted to hear. In any event, the jury did not accept this in mitigation, and Stevens went to the gallows."

"I sometimes wonder," I said, "if killers like Stevens, and the Ripper, are not somehow harbingers of the nature of crimes to come."

"Watson! The evening is yet young, and you and Murray have, I fancy, much more to tell each other. Have another cigar, and I'll pour you both another brandy, and we shall forget for a while the dark and evil deeds of which humanity is capable."

Murray and I left at 11:30, and as he saw us to the door, Holmes said, "Let us not forget the words of *Havamal*."

"'*Havamal*'?"

"*The Words of the High One*, an ancient Viking poem: '*Do not let the grass grow on the paths between the houses of friends*.'"

Acknowledgements

Thanks must go first to David Marcum, editor of the MX Sherlock Holmes series, for his help and encouragement, which helped me extract more from Watson's tin dispatch box than I would have thought possible, and to Steve Emecz, publisher of the series.

Then to my friends both in the UK and the Czech Republic who have had kind words for my stories, both Holmesian and otherwise: Eva Zahradnickova, Jana Kubesova, Frantisek Holik, Martin Plant, Petra Pachlova, Alan Gray, Tomas Dubeda, Misa Cankova, and (in NZ) Ramsey Margolis. And lastly, to the late Michael Ballard, a good writer and a good friend.

MX Publishing

MX Publishing brings the best in new Sherlock Holmes novels, biographies, graphic novels and short story collections every month. With over 500 books it's the largest catalogue of new Sherlock Holmes books in the world.

We have over one hundred and fifty Holmes authors. The majority of our authors write new Holmes fiction - in all genres from very traditional pastiches through to modern novels, fantasy, crossover, children's books and humour.

In Holmes biography we have award winning historians including Alistair Duncan. Brian Pugh and Maureen Whittaker who have all won the Sherlock Holmes Book of The Year Award.

MX Publishing also has one of the largest communities of Holmes fans on Facebook and Twitter under @mxpublishing.

MX is a social enterprise that has raised over $130,000 for good causes including Happy Life Mission (Kenya), Undershaw School for children with learning disabilities (UK) and the WFP (World Food Programme).